SCHLOCK

FEATURING

RUSSIA COP

DAVID R. LOW

SCHLOCK

FEATURING

RUSSIA COP

Kharms & Bowler Publishing

SCHLOCK
Featuring Russia Cop

This book is a work of fiction. Names, characters, businesses, organizations, places, events, and incidents are either the product of the author's imagination or are used fictitiously. Any resemblance to actual persons, living or dead, events, or locales is entirely coincidental.

Kharms & Bowler Publishing

ISBN: 978-1-7362773-1-7

First Edition, 2021

Cover design by Alfred Obare
Book design by Jonas Perez Studio

BOOKS BY DAVID R. LOW

CoinciDATE

SCHLOCK
Featuring Russia Cop

For M.S., J.B., and R.E.

Thanks for showing me the meaning of schlock

Table of Contents

Цой жив

Tsoi Lives

"It's like his voice is underwater. But not quite like that. It's like it's emerging from underwater, or from a separate ethereal plane of existence altogether."

That was the first time I had ever heard about Viktor Tsoi.

It was also the first time I met Hirata.

Hirata moved to Tokyo from some unremarkable village in Iwate Prefecture when he was eighteen. As far as any of us knew, he had no friends, no family, and had arrived in the capital with a cheap guitar that was missing its top and bottom E strings.

I blinked. I was nearly out the door when the dreaded voice came.

"Takahiro!"

"Yes?"

"Were you thinking of leaving with that catastrophe on your desk?"

I turned and blinked.

"How many times have I told you not to blink so much?"

Some of my coworkers had been given permission to leave, while others had managed to sneak out. Most of them were still present. I hurried back to my cubicle, pushed my chair—neatly this time—under my desk, and walked once more toward the exit, where I stopped to bow before my boss.

He did not give the all clear.

A glance back at my desk revealed the culprit—a stray pencil left in the center of the blotter rather than replaced in the adjacent holder.

~~~

A week and two days ago marked one year since I began working for the company, and four years since I had come to Tokyo. Before that, home was a place called Shiogama, in Miyagi. My father, a fisherman, was somewhere between disappointed and
~~~

appalled when I told him I would not be spending my life on a boat, but planned instead to head to the capital.

"Tokyo smells," my mother had said, doing her best to dissuade me. "There's no nature. The people are not kind. Always in a hurry. And where will you get *zunda*? You won't find any in that place."

I worked in Shinjuku. Shinjuku was noise. The sound of life. The constant clicking and clanking of pachinko parlors, arcades, and restaurants. Music playing from a hundred or more different establishments. And people. So many people. People in a hurry. People looking for fun. People like me, in awe of the skyscrapers and bright neon lights of pink and purple.

After finally escaping work that evening, I left the neon lights behind for something darker, more raw. I arrived in Kabukicho around ten o'clock. The Golden Gai, its lantern-lit alleyways glinting with the moisture of recent rain, was famous for its compact bars—typically sitting a maximum of eight people, with some holding as few as four.

The cold January weather had done little to discourage flocks of tourists, almost always louder than groups of even the most exuberant locals, who gawked at the famed minibars—nearly two hundred in all. I passed one where the owner was trying to explain to a white couple that no females were allowed inside.

On this night, by my estimation, tourists outnumbered Japanese five to one.

I had no preference for any particular establishment. I required only drink and noise. All beer tasted the same to me. If it was cold and not too cheap, I found a way to enjoy it. The noise was to drown out the endless stream of thoughts in my head. I was no fan of rock music, but the rowdiest—and therefore most appealing—option was a dingy karaoke bar where a white guy was singing some classic rock ballad from the seventies. I vaguely recognized the tune but didn't know the name or the artist. In front of the tiny corner stage stood the performer's most ardent admirers, a pair of fiftysomething Japanese men decked out in studded leather.

The place was packed body to body, but I managed to grab a beer and slide into an empty table along the back wall, by the old jukebox, which still played on occasion, and where the right song played at the right time on the right night could inspire an impromptu bar-wide singalong.

I scanned the room, noting, as I often did, what others were drinking. Americans, for example, seemed usually to prefer beer to most other options. At the table next to me sat another lone Japanese minding his own business. Whiskey, dry. Beyond him, gathered around a larger table, was a foursome of white guys, shouting their conversation, and thus drowning out the music. I failed to understand why foreigners were always so loud, oblivious to those around them.

Then again, noise was what I came in for.

I had been chastised by my boss before, but today hit differently. The consequence for the wayward pencil? A thirty-minute lecture on poor work attitudes. He stopped short of naming names, but those within earshot knew who carried the brunt of the insults.

The bartender, ever vigilant in spotting misery, brought me another drink.

At the bar sat a bored-looking Japanese around my age—twenty-two—with a guitar strapped and hanging low on his back, its headstock nearly scraping the floor. His hair was a tangled mess, his clothing tired and out of fashion. His guitar looked as neglected as he did.

While my attention caught constantly on the movements and conversations of surrounding patrons, this kid, face blank, stared only forward.

When the last karaoke contender stepped down from the stage, the quad of white guys stood and walked out, leaving only a few stragglers in the place—locals and foreigners alike.

The jukebox kicked in, playing some poorly produced song from the eighties. Primitive guitar, drum machine. The vocalist, singing in neither English nor Japanese, caught my ear. The faces around me faded until all that was left was the youth with the guitar and the voice coming out of the jukebox.

The kid's head turned toward the old machine. What he was taking from that voice, I couldn't say. It looked almost religious. To me it was alien—too strange to be pleasurable. And because I couldn't understand the lyrics, the song's meaning was lost on me.

The kid's body grew rigid, as if suddenly possessed. He leaned over the bar and asked the bartender the title of the song.

The bartender tilted his head in confusion.

As the thin tones of guitar faded and the drum machine slowed, the kid slid off his barstool, made his way to the jukebox, and hunched over the thing.

He then straightened and turned, making a beeline for me. "Pen! Pen!" he said, eyes nearly crazed.

"Eh?"

"Pen," he said. "I need a pen!"

I reached inside my briefcase and withdrew one of several medium-tip black ballpoints and held it out—too slow for the kid's liking, apparently.

He ripped it from my grasp and scribbled the title down

on a damp napkin he'd swiped from a neighboring table. He then exhaled, his shoulders relaxing, and returned the pen.

"You must really like that song," I said.

"Didn't you hear it?"

"I heard it."

"It was so raw. So visceral. Like nothing I've ever heard before."

"So you could understand the words?"

"Not a one. I don't know what the guy was singing about. But his voice. It's like his voice is underwater. But not quite like that. It's like it's emerging from underwater, or from a separate ethereal plane of existence altogether."

"Interesting way of describing it."

"If only I could read what this said." He stared down at the napkin.

"Is that Russian, maybe?" I asked.

He tilted his head and brought a closed fist to his chin. He knew about as much as I did. After that, he seemed to focus on whatever was unfolding inside his head.

I would have attempted more conversation, but I was tired and decided to call it a night. I figured that was the last I'd see of the guy. I didn't even get his name.

~~~

Home, in my mind, was a place for sleeping and eating only. I never invited guests, and once awake, I didn't want to be there.

At 4.5 tatami mats, my room was a tad cramped.

My life consisted of a standard routine. Up by five, and then some gentle morning stretches and crunches. I considered briefly
~~~

the idea of a morning jog, but then I would get no sleep at all.

Breakfast was a light affair: black coffee, toast, orange juice. Anything more than that resulted in severe stomach distress.

By seven, I was on the subway—an eleven-minute walk from my apartment. Wearing a three-piece suit, even in the cool morning air, I was usually drenched with perspiration by the time I arrived at the station. Add to that the combined body heat of several dozen people crammed into the train cars like so many sardines, and my profuse sweating became unbearable. There were plenty of guys who showed up at the office fresh, cool as cucumbers. Unfortunately, I could not be counted among them.

By eight sharp, I was at my desk. No catching my breath. No cooldown period. No time to ease into the day and mindset. We were required to be present for morning announcements, and the workday concluded exactly twelve hours later.

But this is not to say we were allowed to leave at that hour. Life was happening outside…

The boss had several favorites in the office. If he wasn't shooting the shit with one of them, he was shooting the shit on the phone until a quarter to nine. No one was allowed to leave until he emerged from his office for the day.

Only then was it Nomikai time.

After hours, big deals were celebrated—once a twice-weekly thing that quickly became a three-times-a-week thing. Always at one of two local places. Luckily, the boss was a lightweight, and we were set free by eleven.

Still, those were hours I would never get back.

My options after that were to grab a meal from a convenience store near home, or carry on drinking by myself.

If I chose home, I tried to catch up on baseball. My permanent state of being was exhaustion, however, so often even the highlights were too taxing for my brain.

It had been nearly four months since I'd seen any of my school chums—most in similar boats as me, save for the lucky one or two who had found themselves a partner.

One week after my prior visit, I headed back to the karaoke bar, where again I spotted the unkempt kid with the ramshackle guitar. The song—the one he had been so enamored with—was playing on the jukebox. This time, the kid was standing on the little stage, playing and singing along.

The other patrons, most of them tourists tonight, were indifferent, but the kid's passion for the music was palpable. I couldn't be sure if he knew the words he was singing, but nonetheless, it was clear he meant every one of them.

He had caught the attention of a Japanese girl who wore a matching skirt and jacket in a shade of emerald green caught intermittently by the minimal lighting above. She looked out of place among the foreigners.

Nothing, it seemed, could break her gaze from the kid.

She smiled as he delivered the indecipherable lyrics, and her head bobbed in awkward, poorly timed rhythm. Her hair, dark brown with a natural auburn tint, was bobbed neatly at her chin—a somewhat weak chin that would have looked wrong on any other but suited the girl, whose skin was slightly pale. Nothing could divert her attention from the singer, which meant I could stare at her without fear of getting caught.

When the performance came to an end, she was the only person in the room to put her hands together, but her enthusiasm more than made up for that.

The kid threaded his way to the bar, handed the guitar to the bartender, and took a seat two stools down from the girl.

I stepped up behind him. "You've really taken to that song, haven't you?"

"Yes."

The girl leaned over the empty stool between them. "That was awesome."

"Thank you."

"What language was that?" she asked.

"Russian," the kid replied.

"And the singer's name?" I said. "Remember? I gave you the pen to write it down."

"Viktor Tsoi. The band is called Kino. It means 'cinema' in Russian."

A brief silence followed the exchange, during which the girl looked eager to say something but remained close-lipped.

"Shall we introduce ourselves? What is your name?" I glanced at the boy with the shaggy hair, when really, I was more focused on the girl.

"Hirata," he replied.

"I'm Takahiro." I gave a slight bow. "*Yoroshiku.*"

"*Yoroshiku.*" The kid bowed in return.

"I'm Mitsuko," the girl said. "*Yoroshiku onegaishimasu!*" She offered a slightly more enthusiastic bow.

"Do you understand the lyrics?" I asked.

"Yes."

"You taught yourself Russian?"

"Yes."

"Amazing!" Mitsuko said.

I signaled the bartender. "Maybe we should get some drinks?"

We ordered a round of highballs and watched as one of the tourists sang karaoke—a string of Lady Gaga songs, starting with the obligatory "Bad Romance."

Hirata, to my surprise, came alive after a couple of drinks. "You see," he said, "in the Soviet Union, they didn't have ready access to rock music. Literature, film, music—it was all heavily censored. If someone wanted to get their hands on a rock album, they had to pay for it to be smuggled by way of the black market. That's what makes Tsoi so special. Look at a band like The White Stripes. They had decades of influence to pull from. As did AC/DC before them and Led Zeppelin before them. Tsoi and Kino, they didn't have that. He and his band were essentially inventing rock and roll from scratch based on what they imagined it should sound like."

"You really like their stuff, don't you?" I asked.

Hirata nodded.

Mitsuko drained the last of her second highball. "It's late. I should probably go home."

"What?" I said. "You can't go. We're still celebrating Viktor Tsoi. I know another bar we can go to, not far from here."

She eyed me for a moment, then smiled. "Okay. One more drink."

Truth was, I hadn't been this attracted to a woman in a long time. I didn't want to see Mitsuko go, but I also had no game plan, other than playing up Hirata's fascination with Viktor Tsoi. For the moment, I couldn't imagine what we'd possibly have to talk about, but I was confident, sort of, that I'd come up with something on the way to the next venue.

Hirata remained quiet while we traversed the crowded, narrow Kabukicho alleyways. After multiple incidents bumping shoulders with foreigners, I grew irritated. The first two times I could forgive, but by the third, it felt personal.

The bar where we ended up—a typical *izakaya* where the only seating was a counter that wrapped around the kitchen—I'd never been to. This became obvious when the clientele turned to stare at us newcomers—nay, intruders—who had dared walk inside.

The hard-faced, middle-aged owner looked up from behind the bar. "*Irasshaimase*."

Among those seated—all regulars, no doubt—was an elderly man excitedly showing off the prizes he had won from a pachinko machine. I often wondered what kind of old man I'd be. Would I smile? Would I be frail and crass?

We squeezed in between another older gentleman and a salary man nursing a beer. The enticing smell of ramen wafted out from the kitchen, and most of the establishment's patrons were happily slurping up noodles from bowls already set before them.

We split a single bottle of beer between us and cheered once more for Viktor Tsoi.

"What does he look like?" Mitsuko asked. "Is he handsome? Can you show us?"

Hirata shook his head. "I don't have a phone."

"Oh," she said, looking sheepish.

"I can take a look." I pulled my smartphone from my jacket pocket. "How's it spelled?"

To my surprise, the face that came up on my mobile screen didn't resemble what I figured a Russian ought to look like. In fact, I would say he looked a bit like—

"Hirata-kun!" Mitsuko exclaimed. "He looks just like Hirata-kun!"

The resemblance, while not quite uncanny, was there. Similar bone structure and eyes. The hair was off, but if Hirata felt inclined, he could probably grow it out to match Tsoi's.

"He doesn't look all that Russian, does he?" I asked.

"Tsoi's father was Korean," Hirata said. "A Korean born in Soviet Kazakhstan. Imagine that? Russia's most famous rock star was an Asian!"

"Is he really their most famous?" Mitsuko asked.

"Without question," Hirata returned.

I tilted my head. "And how's that?"

"The music, first and foremost. No one sounded like him. Second, despite Soviet censors, he went on to become a national phenomenon. There was no stopping it. He and his band went from underground, playing small gigs and recording DIY in their apartment, to becoming a stadium sensation. They even wrote songs during perestroika, demanding change. That might seem quaint and not all that radical to us, but for a Russian band during Soviet times to openly sing about change, that's pretty extreme."

"Is he still making music?" Mitsuko asked.

Hirata downed the last of the beer. "He died in a car crash when he was twenty-eight."

The three of us went quiet for a time until Hirata spoke again.

"In Moscow," he said, "there's a wall dedicated to him, where fans leave cigarettes and beer."

"Another beer, please!" I called to the owner. "And a curry ramen!"

The noodles were instant, but it didn't matter. The smell of warm curry nearly sobered me. I filled my companions' glasses and proposed one more toast to the Russian Korean Viktor Tsoi.

"I'm sorry, but who is Viktor Tsoi?" asked a round-faced man, perhaps one or two years older than myself, sitting a few stools down.

As Hirata explained, I decided to step outside for a cigarette and asked Mitsuko if she'd care to join me.

She smiled and declined.

Damn.

Others were smoking inside, but I could only listen to the origins of the Korean Soviet legend so many times. I pulled out a pack of Seven Stars, lit one up, and embraced the night. I liked this place—dark and quiet.

A stray tabby padded up to me, and I scratched the top of its head. Perhaps it, too, was a regular at this place. An eruption of laughter from inside the bar broke the silence, scaring the cat off into the night.

I put out my cigarette and walked back inside.

Everyone in the place was in good spirits, and Hirata, it appeared, was the center of their attention. The round-faced man had moved closer, and Hirata was teaching him some Russian words, laughing at the man's attempts to pronounce them.

"*Vashe pivo.*" The owner set a beer in front of Round-face.

Hirata's eyes lit up. "Takeshi-san, you know Russian?"

"I know those two words," Takeshi said. "I was in Russia back in the nineties."

"Do you know of Tsoi?" Hirata asked.

"Can't say I do. But I see you're very passionate about him. Do you have a guitar?"

Hirata's face went dark, and he shook his head.

"But I saw you with a guitar," I said.

"It was stolen."

"Saigo," Takeshi said, "watch the bar."

"*Hai.*"

Takeshi disappeared into a room at the back and returned, brandishing an acoustic guitar. It looked a bit worse for wear, but all the strings were accounted for, at least. He held it out to Hirata, who hesitated at first to take it. Takeshi's subtle nod was an indicator that he must. Hirata held it as if grasping a sacred artifact. I had seen people handle babies with a less delicate touch.

"It only collects dust here," Takeshi said. "It's yours on one condition: you promise to play it every single day."

Hirata rapidly nodded his head.

~~~

The following week, my parents visited. Mom had brought so many zunda-related snacks my room could barely fit them.

"How can you live like this?" Mom said upon seeing the 4.5 tatami mat space. "This is a catastrophe."

"It's a place to sleep," I said.

"A place to sleep," she repeated. "Certainly not a place to live. I've seen rats who live better than this. Are you eating?"

I nodded.

"No, you're not. Look at him," she turned to my father.

My father looked at me.

"Let me make you something."

She opened a cabinet to reveal the last remaining cup of instant noodles.
~~~

"If we came ten minutes later, you'd be dead. We need to go shopping."

Getting out of my place was a relief for me and my mom alike. Discovering my quiet suburb did not; in fact, smell made her relatively more at ease with her son being in Tokyo. However, the products available at the grocery store did not impress her, nor did the prices meet her approval, but she found sufficient ingredients to make nikujaga. It was the best meal I'd tasted in years.

The day after, I fell ill with food poisoning. During my delirium and sleepless nights, I lamented not asking Mitsuko for her number. I had waking dreams of her writing down a series of digits, but they dissolved each time I tried to make sense of them. Hirata didn't even have a phone.

Once I felt human again, I returned to the karaoke bar—a shot in the dark. They weren't there. I waited around forty-five minutes or so before concluding they were unlikely to show, and so up and down Kabukicho I went, looking for any signs. After several passes, I realized I was drawing the attention of promoters handing out flyers for maid cafés and brothels and hostess clubs and soaplands. I waved them off. Uproarious laughter shook the night as two hostesses on the wrong side of thirty walked out of one of the shadier establishments. On their heels were several middle-aged tourists, German by the looks of it. One of the more eager and pudgy Germans kept trying to steal a kiss from one of the hostesses. She laughed at each attempt. Each rejection only seemed to make him more eager to keep trying. His friends encouraged him to give it another go. Going into the establishment were two much younger-looking women, which immediately caught the attention of the Germans. The older hostesses lit up some cigarettes.

Exhausted and not fully recovered from my illness, I decided to head home. I checked my phone; it was half-past midnight. The last train for the night had departed. My only option was to find a 24-hour Internet Cafe and stay there until morning. It was naïve to think I could find Mitsuko again by walking up and down the streets of Kabukicho. The German had a better chance of finding love from a hostess. I was ready to admit defeat.

It was then that I heard two familiar voices drifting out from an unremarkable corner. Tsoi's and Hirata's.

Or, rather, Tsoi from Hirata.

Inside the dingy, poorly lit bar stood Hirata, on a makeshift stage, belting his heart out. His hair was styled as Tsoi's was back in the day, and he was strumming Takeshi's dusty old guitar as if to kill it. He would later tell me the song—the one we first heard at the karaoke bar—was called, "Close the Door Behind Me, I'm Leaving."

I walked inside and slipped onto an empty barstool, immediately catching the warm, familiar smile of Mitsuko, who sat two seats down, closer to the stage. She looked out of place amid the grime and the gritty clientele, but it didn't seem to bother her. She was even lovelier than the first time I saw her, wearing a simple, red fitted shirt, a skirt, and a black fabric necklace, on which hung a pearly oval-shaped stone. Her hair looked recently trimmed.

Between the two of us, I realized, sat Round-face, who turned to me and introduced himself as Yoshiro. It appeared the two were together, as well as accompanied by two others I didn't recognize.

When Hirata's performance concluded, Mitsuko and Yoshiro stood and applauded.

Mitsuko turned to me and smiled. "You came!"

I nodded in response.

"This is Manami-chan," she said, indicating the cute girl to her right. "Next to her is Shin-kun."

Manami had an intelligent face. I figured her for a model student—a class rep, I'd be willing to bet. Shin, by contrast, wore a wide-eyed expression that suggested he hadn't been out in a while, maybe in his entire life. Whereas Hirata was contemplative in his quietness, Shin gave off serial killer vibes. He was so insular in fact, that I often wondered if I ought to remind him to blink, let alone breathe.

Hirata, joining us at the bar, did not acknowledge my presence.

With the stage now empty, music played over the sound system.

"This place is expensive." Yoshiro eyed the highball in front of him as if the drink itself were to blame. Adding to his disappointment, the pack of Echoes, which he drew from his shirt pocket, turned out to be empty.

"Everywhere is expensive," Manami said.

Yoshiro cocked an eyebrow. "You didn't even order anything."

"Because it's expensive."

"I thought you offered to pay for my drink?"

"Me?" Manami pointed at herself.

"We can go to my place," Hirata said, holding up a set of keys.

"Your place?" I said.

Not ten minutes later, we were back at Takeshi's, where Hirata used the keys to let himself in through the back and into a sparse room with a thin mattress on the floor and a small wooden desk.

"Takeshi-san can't afford to pay me, but in exchange for helping him run the place, I get to stay here—food and beer included." Hirata slipped back through the door into the restaurant and returned, carrying three bottles of beer in each hand.

"This is the greatest thing that's ever happened," Yoshiro said, lowering himself onto the mat.

Hirata handed me a beer. "Can I see your phone?"

"Sure."

Soon, the music of Viktor Tsoi filled the little room. "Spring," was the name of the song, according to Hirata. I couldn't say I loved Tsoi's music, but the tune was soothing and easy enough to listen to. For the moment, I was happy. No work, no boss, no bills, no pain. Everyone, in fact, seemed happy, despite the cramped, hot space.

Mitsuko dropped down beside Yoshiro. "Isn't this wonderful?"

I nodded.

"I can't remember the last time I drank this much, though," she said with a giggle.

"What do you do, Mitsuko-chan?" I asked.

"What's your blood type?" she asked.

"Me?"

She nodded.

"I'm blood type A. What about you?"

"I imagine Hirata-kun is blood type O. Don't you think so?"

"What do you do, Mitsuko-chan?" I asked once more.

"I'm an administrative assistant."

"Like answering phones, taking messages, data entry, stuff like that?"

"Yeah, stuff like that."

I had tried before to imagine what kind of job she held, and I could see her working at such a position—organized and capable. Yes, it made sense. What made less sense was her penchant for frequenting the bars of Kabukicho and hanging out with weirdos like Hirata.

"What did you study at uni?" I asked.

"European art history."

"Is that right?" I knew of Picasso and Leonardo da Vinci. But if one were to question me on styles, names of periods, and who came before who, I could not confidently offer any answers.

"Have you ever been to Europe?" I asked.

She shook her head and took a sip from her beer.

She could talk about anything, and I'd happily listen. What's your go-to brand for ink? What's the biggest dog you've ever seen? Tell me your thoughts on pavement, Mitsuko. She noticed I was looking at her slightly longer than I should have been.

Mitsuko. I was in love with her.

I only wish I could offer her something of myself the way Hirata had offered Tsoi to us.

I blinked. The door opened and in breezed a stranger—well-dressed, perhaps a year or two older than myself, eyes glued to his phone. His smile was practiced and his haircut expensive. Clearly he spent ample time in front of the mirror, perfecting his look.

Mitsuko's eyes lit up at the sight of him, and soon she was on her feet, practically throwing herself into the guy's arms.

She turned to the rest of us. "Everyone, this is my boyfriend Ken."

Ken pointed to my hat. "You a Rakuten Eagles fan?"

I nodded.

"I know Masahiro Tanaka," he said. "We just had lunch last week, in fact."

"Oh, stop talking about that," Mitsuko said.

"What?" Ken shot back. "Guy's an Eagles fan. Probably gets a kick out of this stuff."

I nodded.

"See?" Ken gave Mitsuko a squeeze. "The second time we got lunch, some of the girls from Momoiro Clover Z showed up. That was fun. Tanaka's a big fan of their music."

"Working at an ad agency has its perks, I guess," Mitsuko said.

"Where do you work?" Ken asked me.

"I—"

"Bananaman!" Ken exclaimed, his attention abruptly turning to Yoshiro.

Yoshiro's brow shot up. "Eh?"

"Bananaman!" Ken was referring, I assumed, to the popular comedic duo. "You look just like that one guy."

"Shitara-san?"

"No, man. Not the handsome one."

"You mean Himura-san?"

"Yes!" Ken said. "The fat one!"

Manami laughed. "Yoshiro-kun even has the same hair as him!"

Yoshiro, his face red with humiliation, stormed out of the little room.

Ken gestured to my phone on the desk. "What's with this music?"

"It's Tsoi," Mitsuko said.

"What the hell is Tsoi?"

"It's what we listen to here," Mitsuko said.

Ken wrinkled his nose. "I'd rather listen to something I can understand. What's wrong with AKB48?"

"Pop idol bullshit," Hirata offered quietly.

Manami clasped her hands in front of her. "I love AKB48!"

"It's their videos that are interesting," Ken said.

"There is a video where the girls are in a bath together." Shin's first comment of the night and it's unclear whether it was meant to be one of approval or disgust.

"'Ponytail and Scrunchie!'" Manami exclaimed. "I love that song!"

"It's settled, then," Ken said. "Let's put on music we can all enjoy."

Turned out, Ken could talk about himself even more than Hirata could talk about Tsoi. Even baseball, usually one of my favorite topics, became insufferable coming out of Ken's mouth. Still, it felt good to be at Hirata's, and it felt good to be in love. Even Mitsuko having a boyfriend didn't diminish my feelings for her. I wanted only to be near her.

Oddly or not, when I went home that night, I felt uncomfortable masturbating to thoughts of her. Try as I might to picture Mitsuko naked, I imagined instead the two of us walking side by side in a park somewhere, possibly another country. Reaching for her hand was both exciting and terrifying.

It was as if Hirata's place was a separate plane of reality, existing only for us. Beyond Kabukicho. Beyond Tokyo. Where the beer tasted better and where Tsoi's music soared higher than it ever did in those dank dive bars.

Even the days following, at work, couldn't bring down my spirits.

"Your attitude is poor and your performance sloppy," the boss would tell me. "You're going to have to fix that."

"Hai!"

No matter what shit the guy threw my way, I remained happy. Happy because Hirata's place was always there, waiting. On weekdays, the place was fairly quiet, though occasionally Yoshiro or Shin might pop in. On weekends, however, we all gathered. Sometimes even a new face or two would come and then go. Having a place to ourselves was sacred, and Hirata, to his credit, never seemed to mind if any of us showed up unannounced.

Once I stopped in to find Hirata and Shin watching a movie on Shin's laptop. It was no surprise the movie starred Viktor Tsoi.

"What's this one, then?" I asked.

Hirata, eyes fixed to the screen, remained silent.

"*The Needle*," Shin said.

"Any good?"

Shin tilted his head in reply.

I took a seat on the mat beside them. The premise seemed pretty straightforward: Tsoi exacts justice on some thugs supplying drugs to his ex-girlfriend, and he kicks some ass in multiple, not-too-shabby fight scenes. The end of the film, though, left the biggest impression: Tsoi, out walking the streets on a snowy night, is approached by a man who asks for a light. When Tsoi turns to oblige, the stranger thrusts a knife into Tsoi's gut and then walks off. As the scene comes to a close, "Gruppa Krovi," the band's most famous song, plays. Tsoi, bleeding from the wound, lights himself a cigarette and walks off into the night, his image eventually obscured by falling snow. It's uncertain whether he will live or die.

"That's how I want to die," Hirata said.

~~~

On another evening, when we were all there, Hirata picked up his guitar and started strumming and singing. This happened so often that we barely paid attention. Often performing for the restaurant's patrons, he had become something of a staple at Takeshi's. The song he played to us on this particular night, while melancholy, possessed a tinge of optimism. More impressive than his guitar playing, however, was Hirata's voice. The guy could sing—and in a foreign language, no less. While the drinking and conversations went on, the others joking and laughing away, I just listened.

When the song ended, I asked, "What's that one about?"

"Being far, far away," Hirata said. "A place where one has no worries, no problems."

"Do you believe such a place exists?"

"Tsoi sang about it." He brought a cigarette to his mouth.

"Hirata-kun!" Manami said. "Don't move!"

We all froze while she snapped a photo.

"You look so cool in that pose," she said.

"Like Tsoi?" Hirata asked.

Manami grinned. "Just like Tsoi."

"Stay in that pose all the time and you'll always be Tsoi
~~~

in our eyes," Mitsuko said.

It only took Yoshiro half a beer to get drunk, but he rarely stopped there. He was quite entertaining when he drank, and I imagined no one knew this about him, including Yoshiro himself, before he had met us. After three beers, his face grew red, he'd start to sweat, and Yoshiro the salaryman would cease to be until morning, having been replaced by Yoshiro the drunken legend. I liked to think our group gave him a safe haven, free of judgment, to be and act as he liked. Most recently, he had been trying to do something new with his hair—to no avail, I'm afraid.

He scooted close to me, spilling beer from his glass onto his shirt. "You know, when I first met Shin, I thought he was a serial killer."

I chuckled. "You don't say?"

"And now that I've gotten to know him," he continued, "I see I was one hundred percent correct."

"How can you be so sure?"

"Ito-san stopped coming to Takeshi-san's," Yoshiro said, spitting with the words. "She'd been coming here every day after work for eleven years, no fail. But after Shin started showing up, she suddenly vanished. Haven't seen her since."

"You might be onto something there," I said with a nod.

Yoshiro pulled out a pack of Echoes and lit one without offering one to me. "I wanted to ask you something, Takahiro."

"I'm listening."

"Are you listening?"

"Yes."

"It's about a girl."

My eyes reflexively found Mitsuko, whose eyes were fixed on Ken, who was talking and talking and talking some more.

"She has a boyfriend," I said. "As you can see."

Yoshiro's face fell. "She does?"

"He's here all the time."

"He is?"

I gestured discreetly toward Ken.

"No, man," Yoshiro said, too loudly, then leaned in closer. "I'm talking about Manami-chan."

In truth, I had completely forgotten about Manami.

"Manami-chan? I thought you didn't like her."

"What? Wait. Did she tell you something?"

"No, no." I shook my head. "I just never really thought about her, I guess."

"Good," he said. "I don't want you thinking about her because I do, in fact, like her. A lot."

"So what are you waiting for?" I asked. "Make a move."

"Make a move. Right." He sniffed and took a drink from his glass. "Like I have any idea what to say to her. Everything that comes into my head sounds stupid. And now she knows I look like Himura-san."

"Yeah," I said.

"Have you noticed she barely drinks?" Yoshiro said. "At first I thought if I drank more it would be easier to talk to her. But that plan's been a total bust. She never laughs at any of my jokes."

"Why don't you just tell her how you feel?"

He stared at me. "You really are an idiot, aren't you?"

Ken was getting handsy with Mitsuko, whose laughter carried across the room.

I left Yoshiro's side and approached Hirata, who looked particularly gloomy this evening. "What's bothering you?" I asked.

"I'm in Japan."

"Yeah," I said, not following. "Me too. Yoshiro as well."

"I need to be in Russia."

"Russia?"

"Yeah, Russia," he said. "Here, there is no real appreciation for Tsoi's music—or any music, for that matter. In order to feel it, to *really* feel it, I need to go to Russia."

"Have you got any money?"

"Not at the moment. But most nights, I can get by on two hours' sleep. Takeshi-san can't pay me for working here, but if I can get a couple of part-time jobs on the side and work five months straight, I could afford the trip."

"A genius idea!" Yoshiro nodded to Hirata and addressed the group. "Did you hear that, all? We're going to Russia!"

A round of cheers overtook the little room in the back of Takeshi's restaurant. While Yoshiro likely proposed the idea in jest, the others seemed to take it to heart. For the moment at least, our little group was jubilant.

A song of Tsoi's we all recognized began to play—simple drums, upbeat tempo, catchy chord progression. I didn't much care for Tsoi's slow-to-midtempo stuff, which were somber affairs at best, in my opinion. But this tune I liked. Drew me in. And was quite addictive. Not to mention, easier to dance to.

We all chimed in at the chorus. "*Videli noch*! *Gulyali vsyu noch do utraaaaaaaaaaaad*!"

Hirata translated: "We saw the night, we walked the night, until morning."

"Saw" meaning *experienced* or *a part of* and "walked" meaning *hung out* or *being out and about*. Mostly the lyrics were about having a good time.

The thumping music must have given Takeshi's elderly regulars a collective headache, but we didn't care as we jumped and swayed to the music, moving in spastic, carefree motions that had Yoshiro spilling beer on everyone.

We listened on repeat until night turned into morning.

~~~

I blinked and March became August . . .

The night was sleepless—not so much a matter of me tossing and turning, but of staring at the ceiling as my mind tossed and turned, rapidly looping images in that confused realm of semiconsciousness that contained its own brand of logic that made no sense.

During my school and uni days, my friends and I would congregate and spend hour upon hour of whatever free time we afforded ourselves making "grand plans." Plans we knew on some level would never come to fruition but nonetheless occupied our minds and hearts for weeks, often months, on end.

The fun, we understood, was in the planning, not the execution.

I glanced at my bedside clock. Five hours from now, I would be sitting on a plane headed for Saint Petersburg.

I'd never thought about Russia much. From what I gathered in school, and osmosis, it was big and cold and not very welcoming. Certainly not a place I had dreamed of spending my few precious days of vacation time. I would have preferred to convince the others of a trip to Cuba or Hawaii, or maybe Guam.

But that, of course, would never have satisfied Hirata.

Once Hirata and Yoshiro had started making plans and
~~~

drawing up itineraries, the group became obsessed. No one, save for me, could stop talking about the Russia trip.

A trip I feared—and rightfully so—would someday become a reality.

Hirata was already at Narita Airport when I arrived. I wouldn't have been surprised if he had been there a full twenty-four hours in advance. Besides his guitar, he had packed remarkably light, carrying only one small backpack.

Ken, sitting beside him, was the only one among us to bring a Russian phrase book and was presently making an effort to learn some phrases before our departure.

The dread I felt was palpable.

I had never been to an airport before, but I had seen Narita on TV at least a dozen times. Besides baseball, the only television program I cared for was a reality show where a camera crew sought out non-Japanese-looking people disembarking flights, asking them why they came to Japan. Often foreigners had interesting, even strange, stories to share. In some cases, with permission of course, the crew would follow a subject through his or her stay in the country.

On the program, the airport had seemed so vibrant—alive with humanity, buzzing with activity. All I saw now, however, were sterile, uninviting colors and cold, wide corridors.

Ken, Mitsuko, and Hirata sat together on the plane, whereas I was seated next to an elderly Russian couple that smelled, well, they smelled old. As there was plenty of time, I went over my game plan. I had already researched Saint Petersburg's most romantic restaurants and scenic places to stroll. My strategy was to approach Mitsuko when she was alone, but not to come on too strong. For obvious reasons, it wouldn't work to set things up like a date, so I planned instead to let things play out naturally in the hope she would find pleasure in spending time with me.

After we landed, we were directed to passport control, which turned out to be a stressful affair with signs indicating queues for citizens, diplomats, and tourists. In fact, there were no queues at all, but rather a singular mass of people pushing forward like the tide. When it came my turn, the official stared at me blank-faced, as if I should know without prompting the proper protocol. She spat out something in rapid-fire Russian, and when I responded, confused, she repeated herself—this time faster and louder. After an intense stare down I nodded, smiled, muttered something in English, and she stamped my passport.

One thing none of us had thought through beforehand was where to go once there. Outside the airport, we found ourselves surrounded by a grim landscape that resembled nothing of the splendid canals, boulevards, and churches we had seen in photos. The weather was gray and oppressive. Later, we would learn that Saint Petersburg had only roughly twenty-three days of sun per year, and on that day, the sun had neglected to show for our arrival.

Our hotel, not far from the famous high street Nevsky Prospekt, had a check-in time of three o'clock, and here we were at eleven in the morning, sleep-deprived, hampered with our luggage, and frankly, not smelling too great.

Finding the right vehicle—bus, minibus, or bus-like vehicle—to take us to the city center wasn't easy, and drivers were none too eager to help. We opted for the bus, and though we were politely quiet during the ride, we drew numerous wary glances from the other passengers. The bus transported us to another depot similar to the one we had come from, and luckily, this one had a metro.

"What happens next?" Yoshiro asked. "Just go to the hotel?"

"The Tsoi museum is several metro stops from here, on another island," Hirata said. "We should head over."

"Relax," Ken said. "The museum isn't going anywhere. We should get some food and drinks first. Enjoy the sights."

Hirata's expression wilted. Had it been up to him, he would have traveled here on his own, with no other souls to distract him or prevent him from going where he wanted when he wanted.

The escalator to the underground went down and down. Endless. To our left, locals ran down the thing, skipping two to three steps at a time with seemingly no concern about falling on the sharp-edged steps. People constantly pushed into one another. No one, in fact, appeared concerned about the congested route they were taking to their destination, much less who they had to push around to get there. The only time people gave us any notice at all was to gawk. All pedestrians looked potentially dangerous. Every single one. Was this all there was?

Needless to say, my initial impression of the country was far from favorable.

This was the grand city of literature and art and history? Of Hirata's beloved Tsoi? This sentiment, which had started in the first bus depot, didn't let up while on the metro.

When we emerged from the station at Gostiny Dvor, I was sufficiently humbled.

The sun, having finally managed to sneak out from behind the cloudy blockade, shone forth, though faintly, but enough to reveal Nevsky Prospekt, with its grand boulevards, canals, and colorful European buildings designed and erected with expert precision.

Manami, overwhelmed by the sheer number of sights in our field of vision, pointed her camera in every direction, taking shot after shot. As the onion-domed cathedral of the Church of the Savior on the Spilled Blood came into view, I sensed the others—most of them, anyway, and Mitsuko, in particular—felt, as I did, the power of this magnificent city.

Only Hirata looked on with indifference.

Simply put, the city didn't appear real, seeming instead to reflect some fantasy version of what a European capital was meant to look like.

"Even without having read any Russian literature, this place is still remarkable," Mitsuko said.

"Yes, yes. Dostoevsky. Very nice. Now let's drink," Yoshiro said.

The federal city's main street, Nevsky Prospekt, along with its side streets, seemed comprised mostly of bars—limitless choices. And like a current pushing out to sea, we were carried down the avenue by a wide throng of curiously tall pedestrians.

Manami, eyes darting left and right, hastened her steps to keep up with us. "Even the women are giants," she said with a frown. "And look at all the trash. It's everywhere. It's hard to enjoy the beauty of this place with so much rubbish tossed on the ground."

We settled on a place called Killfish because Shin liked the name.

With luggage in hand, we filed inside and were greeted by a young security guard who seemed to take great pleasure in making the girls empty the contents of their bags. I fought the urge to cover my nose against the foul onslaught; the place reeked of cigarette smoke, stale booze, and body odor. I hefted my pack up at my side as we crossed the sticky floor en route to the counter. With each table we passed, we drew the suspicious eye of locals tending to their beers.

We managed to squeeze between several patrons, who seemed unconcerned about making room for us. The bartenders, for their part, made every effort to avoid eye contact.

We all turned to Hirata.

"Will you order for us?" Manami asked.

Hirata leaned over the counter, managed to hail a server, and rattled off a sentence or two in Russian. I had little on which to base my opinion, of course, but to me, Hirata's Russian sounded great.

The bartender, clearly unimpressed, merely stared at him.

When Hirata tried again, the guy replied, in English. "I not understand you. What does you want?"

"Beer," Hirata said.

"What beer?"

"Unfiltered."

"Do not have."

"Wheat."

"Do not have too."

"Light beer."

To this, a slight nod accompanied by a roll of the eyes.

We passed him our money, and he handed back a receipt. While we stepped away and waited, we watched as others came up to order and then take their receipts and move on. Turned out, there was another, separate counter where we were to retrieve our order—an enormous tank of beer that Hirata plunked in the center of our table.

"This," Yoshiro said, holding up a half-filled glass, "is the single worst thing I have ever put in my mouth. I didn't know it was possible to make something this vile. Oh, look at the menu, they've got sushi. I can only imagine how good it must be here,"

While Yoshiro gave the menu a once-over, Manami snapped some shots of the bleak establishment, drawing attention I would have preferred to avoid.

A broad-shouldered, Adidas-clad Russian man with a black eye and a crooked nose approached and sat down, resting his elbows on the table. "*Nu privet, kitaitsy.*"

I glanced at the others. "What did he say?"

"He said, 'Hi, Chineses,'" Hirata answered.

"Tell him we're not Chinese," Ken said.

Hirata did as requested.

"What is difference?" the Russian said. "I am Artyom. Because you are here, you will drink with us."

"Us?" Yoshiro and I asked in unison.

A second Russian, about the same size and shape as the first, appeared and stated that his name, too, was Artyom.

"Tyoma," Artyom Two said to Artyom One. "What do you think? Do you fancy Chinese chicks?"

"They say they are not Chinese," returned Artyom One.

"Okay. Do you fancy Chinese chicks who are not Chinese?"

"Not sure yet." He returned his attention to us. "You are our guests. Let us drink vodka."

I leaned close to Hirata. "Do we really want to drink with these guys?"

"As our guests, you"—he pointed a finger in turn at

Hirata, Ken, Yoshiro, Shin, and myself—"are obliged to drink with us. It is rude to decline."

"Be men," said Artyom Two. "Make Peking proud."

A server appeared and set a full bottle of chilled, cheap vodka on the table along with seven short tumblers.

Artyom One did the honor of pouring.

That vodka was officially the foulest thing I had ever put in my mouth. Washing it down with the second foulest—the light beer Hirata had ordered—did little to cancel out the taste, and instead produced a toxic combination in my throat.

"So, guys," Artyom One said, "why you come to Russia?"

We all turned to Hirata.

"Do you know the music of Viktor Tsoi?" he asked.

The Russian laughed.

"What is funny?" Artyom Two asked.

"This guy, he asks me if I know Tsoi." Artyom One downed the contents of his glass and brought it down hard on the table. "Yes, I know Viktor Tsoi."

"I like his music," Hirata said. "It's all I listen to. I play guitar and sing his songs. I wanted to come to his country. Maybe see some places where he played."

"Tsoi's music is boring. For old people." The Russian poured another shot from the bottle and tossed it back. "You want good time, listen hard bass. Many great clubs here."

"But Tsoi is what I like," Hirata said.

The Russian sat back with a smirk. "Suit yourself."

~~~

We had been inside Killfish so long I had forgotten what the
~~~

world outside looked like. The sunlight, earlier in the day a hazy affair at best, nearly blinded us as we spilled out onto the sidewalk at three o'clock.

Good and drunk, we made the trek to our hotel and checked in.

"The girls are tired and so am I," Ken said as we started for our rooms. "Give us an hour to rest up, huh? Ninety minutes, maybe?"

I nodded. "I'm a bit jet-lagged myself."

Hirata, frustrated by yet another delay, sulked the rest of the way to our room.

After we let ourselves in, I dropped my bag on the floor, threw myself belly-down on one of the two beds, and closed my eyes. I didn't know whether it was the jet lag, the unfamiliar environment, or Hirata's incessant pacing, but after ninety minutes, I was still awake.

Hirata and I ventured out, getting no response at Yoshiro and Shin's room.

Manami came to her door, eyes half-open, hair mussed. "I think I'm going to stay in, see if I can't sleep off this jet lag."

We tried Ken and Mitsuko.

"Hey, guys," Ken said. "There's a restaurant, Art-Caviar, Mitsuko really wants to go to, so the two of us are headed over there later this evening. You guys have fun. We'll catch up with you tomorrow."

Fuck! Art-Caviar had been on my list of places to take Mitsuko.

"Ninety minutes I waited," Hirata mumbled.

The place, it turned out, was far from the city center and located on one of the islands. For nearly twenty minutes, we combed the residential area, which had no distinctive landmarks to indicate if we were even going in the right direction.

"It was once a boiler house," Hirata explained. "Do you know what Kamchatka is?"

I shook my head.

"It's Russia's most eastern territory on the mainland. This place is named after it. He worked here, three years as a stoker. Eventually he'd bring his guitar and play for those who cared to listen. Soon, he began to develop fans. This was the spot before he became big."

All the buildings in the vicinity looked the same—gray and drab. I was certain we were walking in circles. We approached a duo of teenage Russian males, smoking cigarettes.

"I'll ask for directions," Hirata said.

"Somewhere over there," said one in English, gesturing loosely northeast of where we stood.

"Thanks," Hirata said.

"Where are you guys from?" the friend asked.

"Japan," I said. "Tokyo."

"Why you so interested in the Tsoi?"

"His music is the greatest thing I've ever heard," Hirata said. "Do you like Tsoi?"

The two mates exchanged an amused glance and shook their heads.

"Why not?"

"It is music for old people," said the first.

"Maybe it is old," Hirata said. "But does that make it bad? That he was influential matters, yes?"

The Russian shrugged his shoulders.

"The music is too simple, the lyrics too primitive. It's also derivative of Joy Division, The Cure. The Smiths. I can keep listing them. All better bands."

"Maybe you guys should listen to modern Russian music instead," the second Russian chimed in.

They laughed.

"Don't listen to him," said the first. "Only modern Russian music worth listening to is Alina K."

This time, before Hirata could argue, I pulled him away. "Thank you very much."

Hirata had described the place as a museum, but it wasn't quite that. It was tiny, for one, only slightly bigger than Takeshi's restaurant.

Near the entrance was a small counter manned by a disinterested employee—head bowed, scrolling down the screen of his phone. Pinned up behind the guy was a display of T-shirts featuring Russian rock stars, including Tsoi. The walls on either side were littered with DVDs and CDs, all looking to be bootleg—Tsoi's concerts and other performances, interviews, behind the scenes. There were also newspaper clippings, scraps of clothing, random accessories, and even a guitar.

Behind the museum was a bar and a stage.

I stepped back to let Hirata soak it all in. This is what he came here for. He could take as much time as he needed to get whatever it was he was looking for.

After spending some time in a trancelike state, he approached the guitar, hesitating at first to touch it. He glanced toward the employee, who couldn't be bothered to look up, and then took a chance, wrapping his fingers around the instrument's neck. He touched each string, tenderly, one by one.

I was envious. I wish I cared about anything as much as Hirata cared about Tsoi.

He drew his hand away and turned abruptly. "Will you drink with me?"

I nodded.

We ordered two rancid-tasting dark beers and sat on a rickety wooden bench to the left of the stage.

A couple stragglers shuffled in and took seats on an identical bench opposite us. Shortly after that, three guys showed up and began loading equipment onto the stage. The stage was nearly too small to fit it all, but they managed. I could feel Hirata's heart beating. It was an older crowd—forty-plus—and I knew what Hirata must have been thinking: original Tsoi fans. Those who had, once upon a time, seen the performer in the flesh. Perhaps here, in this very place.

When the band started playing, Hirata became laser-focused, like a cat spotting a mouse.

Several songs in, however, he turned to me and said. "This isn't a Tsoi song,"

I nodded.

"This isn't a Tsoi song," he repeated after the next two songs.

Near the end of the set, which consisted of selections by multiple old-school Russian rock outfits, the band played what turned out to be their one and only Tsoi song. This lifted Hirata's spirits.

After the band made their way down from the stage, Hirata stood and approached the singer, who also played guitar. The guy was smoking a cigarette in a corner and didn't seem too eager for human interaction. His shaggy, mid-length hair—meant, I assumed, to create a younger look—only accentuated his membership in the forty-plus club. His face, red with years of hard drinking, wasn't doing him any favors either.

"Hello," Hirata said.

The man gave a weak nod and took a pull from his cigarette.

"The Tsoi song was really great. Do you guys play any more Tsoi?"

The musician shifted uncomfortably inside his ill-fitting jean jacket, trying in vain to adjust his T-shirt to cover what appeared to be a hard-earned beer belly. "Honestly, man," he said, "we play that song mostly out of obligation. People are tired of Tsoi, and so are we. Akvarium and Nautilus are always a better bet for keeping the crowd with us."

"I think Tsoi is a genius," Hirata said.

The singer shrugged. "To each his own."

"I play guitar and sing his songs."

"In Chinese?"

"I'm not Chinese. And no, I sing them in Russian."

Another shrug.

With the set over, most of the "crowd"—all of fifteen people—left the venue. A few stuck around to chat over drinks. Hirata walked up to a table where a couple of middle-aged rock fans sat. They humored him for a few minutes until the novelty of the young, foreign Tsoi fan wore off and they, too, made to leave.

Hirata returned to our bench and sank down next to me.

"Want to drink more?" I asked.

He gave no indication that he had even heard the question.

"Come on," I said. "The night is still young."

When Hirata remained despondent, I dragged him out of the place, and we rode the metro back to Nevsky Prospekt.

The boulevard was even more active at night than during the day. Women, in particular, were everywhere. Russian women didn't much excite me, nor did white women in general, but they were, in any case, a sight to behold. All dolled up and dressed to the nines, almost to a farcical degree: severe makeup, heels so high, and all wearing broad, bushy coats, both long and short, that made them appear like another species altogether. They caught my attention and that of just about every other passerby, with the exception of Hirata.

We ventured onto a side street and, as it happened, into another realm.

The bright lights of Nevksy dimming in our wake, we moved farther into a stifling darkness that led only to more darkness. Unlike the narrow alleyways of Kabukicho, this was a proper street with plenty of space, seemingly, for pedestrians to walk in either direction.

But for the bodies. A virtual sea of bodies—Russians and tourists, alike. Some conscious, many semiconscious from alcohol consumption, and a few unconscious from what appeared to be severe beatings.

Outside one club, we spotted a meaty bouncer pounding on a scrawny male—Russian, I presumed—as the kid's friends, and even police, looked on.

Large plastic cups—blue, red, clear—littered the pavement. At one point, I watched a drunk foreigner snag a half-empty cup of beer found at his feet and finish it off. His friends clapped and cheered with approval as they continued on.

There were bars aplenty, all dark and cramped, making it difficult to discern which was more desirable than another. After turning a second corner, we came across a small crowd made up of mostly foreigners drinking and smoking outside a joint alive with music. The bouncer, roughly two meters tall and no less than one hundred and forty kilograms, glowered down at us. The kid getting beat up a few blocks back still plenty fresh in our memories, Hirata and I exchanged a nervous glance before asking, with a slight bow, to be let in. The bouncer, satisfied that he had made us sweat, smirked and stepped aside.

There had to be nearly a hundred people crammed inside the tiny joint. Getting anywhere from where we stood seemed impossible, yet people were moving about, in and out. At the back, people were singing karaoke. Without a beat, Hirata and I locked eyes and grinned, each of us feeling a jolt, seeing that machine in some godforsaken bar in Saint Petersburg.

Most of the patrons were singing along with the drunk woman at the mic. Her friends, sitting at a table up front, were particularly enthusiastic—singing the chorus louder than she, while spilling beer and flicking cigarette ashes onto the floor. Nearby, foreigners were happily chatting up local women—though here not nearly the cream of the crop, like I had seen on Nevsky. Most of the locals in the place appeared to be teenagers.

We ordered Johnnie Walker Red.

What we were served was anything but. Barely even whiskey.

Hirata flipped through the massive karaoke songbook, finding songs of mostly American and British artists. Did Russia not have a catalogue of their own music, or did they simply not care to display it?

When it came Hirata's turn, he was pushed back in the queue by an excitable group of twentysomething girls desperate, it seemed, to sing Beyonce's "Love On Top." He let it slide. After the third time of others skipping ahead of him in line, Hirata lost his patience, pointing a finger and letting out a stream of ire. The patrons just laughed, amused by the frustrated Japanese guy yelling in a language they couldn't understand.

When finally his big moment came and Hirata took the mic, only a few patrons even bothered to look up before resuming their drinking. Hirata cleared his throat, and his eyes drifted over the heads of those present, perhaps to Leningrad 1989, to an imaginary audience of adoring fans. Over the PA came a familiar opening guitar riff, followed by electronic drums. "Gruppa Krovi" was the band's most popular song, Hirata had once told me, and the song that had played at the end of that movie we watched, in which it was unclear whether Tsoi lives or dies. The lyrics, like many of Tsoi's, were politically motivated. Specifically, antiwar. The title translated as "blood type." A rarity in Soviet Russia, the song became an anthem for its youth at the time.

When Hirata's vocals kicked in, he drew the brief attention of a local or two, while the foreigners in the place looked either bored or confused.

When the song concluded, Hirata stood.

No applause. Not a single clap.

"Tsoi Zhiv!" One of the locals was on his feet, pointing at Hirata and laughing.

Hirata's face turned to stone. He set down the mic and walked out of the bar, breezing right by me without a word.

I downed the last of the wretched whiskey and hurried out after him.

A moment later, I stood on the sidewalk, dumbfounded. Like a ninja, my friend had vanished into the dark depths of Dumskaya. I took off running—up and down streets, in and out of alleyways—weaving my way in and among the drunken masses.

I returned to Nevsky and did the same, to no avail, before heading back to the hotel.

After finding our room empty, I knocked on Yoshiro and Shin's door.

"I'm sure he's fine," Yoshiro said, still half-asleep. "He'll come back when he's ready."

~~~

By morning, there was still no Hirata.

"He's acting like a baby," Ken said over breakfast. "Running away and ruining our good time by making us worry. If he turns up, fine. If he doesn't, good riddance."

Who even asked you to come?

Mitsuko, at least, accompanied me to the concierge. "If you see him," she said, "could you tell him to please call me?" She pushed a small piece of paper with her number across the desk, to which the receptionist replied with a smile and nod. "This is a city of five million," Mitsuko said after we had all gathered in the lobby. "We're not going to find him by jumping from island to island, shouting 'Hirata!'"

Yoshiro nodded. "He probably just needs some time to cool down. I propose we go out and do our best to enjoy ourselves. Hirata will turn up when he's ready."

Manami's face twisted in concern. "You don't think we ought to file a missing person report with the police?"
~~~

"Come off it," Ken said. "He's just being his usual selfish self. All tortured and morose. He's fine. Let's go. I want to see the city."

I couldn't enjoy the sights, not knowing the whereabouts of my friend. It didn't help that I felt somewhat responsible. Add to that Ken's big mouth, and I was in hell. Our friend was out there alone in a foreign country, and no one seemed all that bothered by it.

When we had walked as far as our legs would take us, Ken and Yoshiro suggested we get drinks. The girls, who weren't in the mood, went shopping instead, stating they would meet us later that evening. We decided on an establishment of slightly higher quality than Killfish, where the beer, though not good, was somewhat more drinkable.

"Let's be real." Ken slurped the foam from the top of his glass. "Do any of us actually like Hirata? More than that, does he even like or care about any of us?"

"What are you saying?" I asked.

"What I mean is, the guy appears not to give a good goddamn about any of us, whether we're around or not. Sure, his place is cool for hanging out and getting drunk. But all he ever does is play that crappy old guitar and blabber on and on about some ancient Russian rock star. Hirata needs an audience. Doesn't much matter who that audience is. Get it?"

"Hirata's my friend," I said.

"Is he?" Ken narrowed his eyes on me. "Seems you're a whole lot more loyal to Hirata than he is to you. You didn't even want to go on this trip."

"I never said that."

"You didn't have to."

I sat back and looked away, folding my arms across my chest.

"I'm sure he'll turn up," Yoshiro said.

Shin looked at the wall.

"I'm sick of talking about Hirata," Ken said. "I'd much rather talk about how unbelievable the women are here. Is it me or is every damn one of them beautiful?"

Ken scanned the women in the room, as Shin continued to look at the wall.

"Yeah, if I weren't already taken," Ken said, "I'd for sure be chatting some of them up. What are you guys wasting your time talking to me for? Get out there and meet some women."

"Maybe they're homos," Shin said.

Ken laughed and left the table, he said, to order another round of beers. He remained at the bar, however, for well over an hour, chatting up the servers, as well as, I noted, several local women.

By the time the girls got back in touch, suggesting we meet them at a new place, Ken had left the bar. I cared less about his whereabouts than he cared about Hirata's.

We met the girls outside a restaurant on Rubinstein Street. Right off, Mitsuko asked about Ken. When I explained he had left the bar without us, she walked off in a huff.

I told the others I wasn't feeling well and went back to the hotel.

~~~

Crack!

I startled awake to the sound of explosions. Had a war broken out?

After another round, I exhaled. Only thunder.
~~~

It was day four of the trip.

When a bolt of lightning lit up the room, a silhouette came into view.

Hirata was perched on the edge of the neighboring bed, cigarette poised between two fingers, just like in the photo Manami had taken.

I bolted upright. "Where the hell have you been?"

"Moscow."

"What? How?"

"I took the overnight train."

"Why?"

"I wanted to see the Tsoi wall on Arbat Street."

"And you didn't bother to tell anyone. Why?"

He stared at me, mystified, as if he didn't understand the question.

I stood and pulled on a pair of jeans. "So?"

"So, what?" He took a long drag and exhaled. "I went to the wall. I left cigarettes and beer. Thought maybe I'd find Tsoi fans there who shared my passion. People I could make a real connection with for once in my fucking life."

"I see." The comment stung, I had to admit. "Um, did it never occur to you that those of us you left behind might be worried about you? That some of us might have even wanted to go with you, see the wall too?"

Another mystified stare.

Accepting the futility, I dropped that line of questioning. "So, did you?"

"Did I what?"

"Did you find anyone there who shares your passion?"

I asked, each word punctuated by my growing irritation—not that Hirata noticed or cared.

He leaned toward the nightstand and dropped his cigarette in a mostly empty bottle of water. "Not one fucking person. Up and down Arbat I went. Bars, clubs, music venues. I'll find a needle in a haystack before I find a single fucking Viktor Tsoi fan in all of fucking Russia." He ran a hand through his hair, which needed a wash even more than it usually did.

"I'm sorry, man." I meant it.

"What's the average Russian life expectancy? Forty, fifty? Perhaps Tsoi's fans all died before he did, or not long after. I feel like I'm the only one in the whole fucking universe who understands the brilliance of his music."

I dropped down on my bed, opposite Hirata. "There's got to be someone else out there."

"Where? Maybe the receptionist. Cool, let me go down and talk to the receptionist. If not her, I'll go to the next hotel, then the next one, then McDonald's. I'll go to every bar and club and shithole on Dumskaya. As a matter of fact, why wait?"

"I don't know. Maybe you could—"

He picked up his guitar and stormed out of the room.

I hurried after, tripping over myself as I struggled to get my feet into my sneakers, and followed Hirata at a distance to Nevsky, where I found him at a busy pedestrian intersection. His playing and singing were unrestrained, rougher than usual—voice cracking, fingers slipping, his passion palpable, bordering on desperate.

Unlike other street musicians, there was no open instrument case or bucket to catch the loose change of passersby. Hirata was playing to play, in the hope of discovering his musical soul mate.

Russians walked past, paying no mind. Tourists too.

Rain began to fall, and fall harder. The thunder resumed, accompanying Hirata's chords. An hour went by, and the sun came out, pushing the rain away, then disappeared again. Hirata's voice was growing hoarse, but there was no point, I knew, in attempting to shake him from his quest.

I returned to the hotel and fell back to sleep. When I awoke two hours later, I found Mitsuko sitting alone at the hotel bar.

"Mind if I sit?"

"Do whatever you want."

"You okay?"

"Ken's cheating on me."

"Are you certain?"

She sipped the clear contents of her glass; Mitsuko was the lone vodka convert in the group. "He isn't exactly subtle. Turns his head at every attractive woman he sees. If that isn't enough, he's been taking off in the evenings, disappearing until late. Comes home reeking of cheap perfume."

"That isn't proof."

"No, it's not," she returned curtly. "But seeing a naked fucking Russian whore in my bed certainly is."

"Whoa."

"Yeah."

"What did Ken say when you found out?"

"He doesn't know I know."

"But you just said—"

"Ken must have been in the toilet when I let myself into our room last night. When I noticed her lying there, bare white ass peeking out of the sheets, I fled the room before either knew I was there."

"Damn, I'm sorry. That must have been really hard."

"You're telling me," she said, taking a swig from her glass. "And if he's cheating on me here, who's to say he hasn't been doing it all along?" Her eyes filled. "God, I feel so stupid!

"Look," I said, "I can't imagine there's anything I could do or say right now to make you feel better. Maybe let's try to enjoy what little time in this city we have."

"I don't know . . ."

"Come on," I said. "What do you have to lose?"

"My boyfriend, apparently," she laughed, despite herself.

"You want to get out of here?" I asked.

"And go where?"

"Don't know, don't care."

She studied my face for a moment. "You're weird."

"I'll take that as a compliment."

"And therein make my point."

This time, it was my turn to laugh.

~~~

It was the first time the two of us had ever walked side by side. My plans for scenic strolls and romantic restaurants had gone out the window. But this was good enough.

"Stop walking so fast," Mitsuko said.

"Sorry," I said, slowing my pace.

"It's okay."

The evening was young, and I felt positive energy all around us. The people of the city, especially the youth, seemed
~~~

in good spirits. But I wondered: Did Mitsuko want to be walking with me or would anyone have done? Better not to know, I decided. What mattered for now was that we were together. I planned to revel in the moment for as long as it existed.

"Where are we going?" she asked.

"I was thinking that place on Rubinstein Street."

"Okay." Her reply was lifeless, passive.

Getting there took us by the intersection where Hirata had been playing. Hours later, he was still there, his fingers bloodied and raw. As it was earlier, people simply flowed past him without even a glance.

Mitsuko came to a halt. "Hirata-kun?"

I explained what had happened and where he'd been.

"That's really sad." Tears welled in her eyes, then ran down her cheeks. "I'm sorry," she said. "I can't do this."

My heart sank as I watched her weave her way back down the sidewalk in the direction of the hotel. Despite my disappointment—or perhaps because of it—I continued on toward the pub, texting Yoshiro on the way.

No response.

Once inside and seated at the counter, I tried Shin: *Want to meet me at the pub on Rubinstein?*

Sure.

Is Yoshiro around?

Saw him heading out with Manami-chan. Not long ago. I'll write him. Okay, bye.

I set down my phone and ordered a beer. Being the only lone patron in the place, I was reminded of my nights spent in the bars of Kabukicho. Back then, I never felt unhappy when drinking by myself. But here in Saint Petersburg, the loneliness was bearing down on me.

I sipped my beer, slower than usual, wanting to wait for the others before tying one on. Thirty-five minutes passed. The pub was a fifteen-minute walk from the hotel, at most. Where was Shin? My beer now gone, I waited ten minutes before ordering another. Halfway into that one, I sent Shin another text.

No response.

~~~

Twenty minutes later, in the hotel lobby, I ran into Yoshiro.

"Where have you been?" I asked.

"What do you mean?" he said. "I was out with Manami-chan."

"Didn't Shin get in touch with you?"

"Not that I know of. Why?"

"He was supposed to meet me at the pub over an hour ago, but he never showed."

We got off the elevator on the fourth floor and rounded the corner. Yoshiro slipped his key card into the slot and, following the click, pushed open the door of their room.

What I saw was something that will be burned into my retinas for the rest of my life. Shin wasn't only home; he had made himself very much at home with Mitsuko atop his face. It would have been one thing to walk in on them having sex, but what I saw was so unexpected and so strangely intimate that my brain couldn't process it. They were quite passionately engaged in the 69 position, with Mitsuko smothering him with her ass. It took the happy couple several seconds to even realize others had entered the room, so I saw vividly what kind of lover Mitsuko was. I saw the way she took Shin's dick in her mouth. For
~~~

months I had dreamed up every possible scenario of what sex with Mitsuko would be like. How it would go down, who would initiate what, what her nipples would look like, what things she'd be into. But I never imagined she'd so enthusiastically 69 someone on the very first intimate encounter with that person, and especially not with Shin of all people. When my eyes locked with Mitsuko's, my stomach lurched and churned. What Yoshiro was feeling in that moment, I couldn't say. But I didn't much care.

I ran out of the room and out of the building, heading straight for the intersection.

~~~

Hirata's voice was barely audible by now and his shirt smeared with blood from ragged hands.

Still fuming and troubled by what I had just witnessed, I marched up to him, mid-song. "You idiot!" I shouted. "What the hell are you doing?"

He continued strumming. "Playing the only music that matters."

"Fucking stop. Just stop! Can't you see you're making a fool of yourself, and for what?" I waved a hand toward the passing pedestrians. "This whole thing has been a giant waste of time."

"Maybe for you."

"What does that mean? What are you going to do? Stand at this intersection and keep playing music no one gives a shit about until someone acknowledges you?"

"Yes."

Blood dripped from the thumb of his right hand, making a teardrop shape on the pavement below.
~~~

"Even if it takes a hundred years?"

"Even if it takes a thousand years. I will stand at this intersection for a thousand years playing until someone acknowledges me, and if after a millennium that doesn't happen, I will go from every intersection from here to Siberia to Sakhalin Island until I find one person who feels what I feel."

"You're insane," I said.

"I'm not, you are. You're the one who wasted months of his life following someone around when he didn't even give a shit about him. Pretending to like the music I liked."

"That's not fair," I said.

Hirata jumped out in front of a passing woman. She nearly jumped out of her skin.

"Tsoi! Viktor Tsoi! Ever heard of him! He's a legend, of course you have!"

She ran away. He turned his attention to a group of teens.

"What about you youngsters? Ever heard of Viktor Tsoi? You know that song that goes like this?"

He started strumming on his guitar and singing incoherently. The youngsters laughed and walked off.

"Here's the problem, I should have seen it," he said. "I am Viktor Tsoi. I am Tsoi reincarnated. I have to struggle as he struggled. Only then will it all make sense. How can I expect these people to know this? Or maybe I have to die again."

Hirata ran up to a Russian couple holding hands.

"Will you please stab me while I walk away listening to 'Gruppa Krovi'?"

The couple walked around him. Hirata ran after.

"I don't think you heard what I'm asking. I want you to

stab me. Once stabbed, I will start smoking and walk off while "Gruppa Krovi" plays. If I live, I'll walk off forever. If I die, I'll wake up as Viktor Tsoi,"

The couple ran off.

"Stop it you fool!" I said.

"You're the biggest fool I ever met," he said.

"How?"

"Let me sing in peace."

"Come home."

"I'm not going back to the hotel."

"Not the hotel, to Japan. Let's get out of here."

Then he replied in one terse, final tone, "I'm never going back to Japan again."

I blinked.

~~~

I'm fifty-six years old now. I work for the same company. My boss is no longer the same man who used to chastise me for leaving a pencil or Post-It note on my desk. My new boss is seventeen years my junior. He's an okay guy, but we have little in common.

I don't know whether Hirata made good on his promise to remain in Russia. I flew back to Japan immediately following our argument at the intersection. I didn't tell the others I had exchanged my ticket for an earlier return date.

The first three weeks back in Tokyo, I went to work and went home. Watched baseball highlights. During the fourth week, I took a chance and returned to Takeshi's—not necessarily hoping, but thinking I might run into Hirata or one of the others. I didn't.
~~~

A year went by, and I stopped in again, asking Takeshi if he had heard anything from Hirata. He simply shook his head.

That was that. I decided to put Hirata and the rest of them out of my mind.

Time went on. I never realized how oppressive time could be. I was aware of it, saw it passing on the face of the clock, but once I turned thirty, I began to realize what it meant.

By thirty-one, I realized those days hanging out with Hirata at Takeshi's place, singing the songs of Viktor Tsoi, learning the history of Soviet rock music, were the greatest days of my life. Rarely do people recognize this when it's happening.

I imagined my greatest days would involve a romance—the kind that occurs in movies. I ventured to believe that it would happen for me. I'd meet a wonderful woman, we would marry, have a couple of kids, adopt a dog, perhaps get a cat. But no. I'm a midlifer now. Never did marry. Seemed like too much effort. Instead, I have devoted most of my time and energy to my work, however thankless. Eventually, the younger guys in the office stopped inviting me to go out—not out of dislike for me, but out of respect, so as not to bother the old man.

It was nearly a decade after the Russia trip when I conceded that the best days of my life had been and gone. Spent gathering at Hirata's, listening to and talking about music and videos with Mitsuko, Manami, and Yoshiro. That was happiness, pure and simple. Hell, even Shin and Ken didn't seem so bad from a distance.

I never figured Tsoi for being the most significant part of my life. When I was around forty, by chance, I stumbled across an article on the anniversary of the songwriter's death. At that time, he had been set to tour Japan and Korea, and had commented that he preferred the Far East to the West, stating that Western journalists were pompous and arrogant and always asked the same banal questions.

Immediately my mind went to Hirata, wondering if he had read it.

I'd like to believe that Hirata eventually found someone who shared his passion and deep appreciation for Tsoi. In truth, none of the rest of us did, and none of us ever truly understood Hirata. We liked that we had a place to drink and be together and talk about music videos. How wonderful that was.

The English Teacher

"Is this everyone?" My attention was not on the audience but on the fresh coffee I had just spilled. While my suit vest hid most of the stain, the white shirt underneath now clung to my torso, soaking my skin and making it impossible to think about anything else. I looked up. "I suppose this is everyone."

Only five students? Last year had been considered a disaster when only eight showed. Once upon a time, nearly twenty students had signed on for the Russian exchange program—a fluke and nothing more. Why anyone at all, let alone dozens, would want to travel to Russia, nay *live* there, was baffling at best. I had had little luck, after all, explaining to peers and colleagues my own experience studying there. Even after I returned home, most presumed I had spent the year in Germany. When I would clarify that, no, I had been in Russia, the typical response was, "Is there a difference?"

So here it was another year and another batch of fresh-faced college students willing to live six months to a year in Russia, with strangers—ones paid to feed and provide beds for adult Americans.

"Thank you for coming," I said to the group. "My name is Marshall, and I'm the study abroad coordinator for Russia and Eastern Europe." But really only Russia; the programs in Poland and Hungary had closed some years back. The university had insisted we continue to refer to the major as

"Slavic Languages and Literature" when, in fact, Russian was the only remaining Slavic language still on offer. "I'm a 2012 alum of the year-long program in Saint Petersburg, and I'm excited to go over everything the program entails. Before we get started, how about you introduce yourselves, give one or two reasons why you chose to study Russian and live a semester or two in Russia?"

A girl with jet-black hair pulled into a tight bun raised her hand. Despite appearing to be under the age of twenty-one, she gave the impression of a seventeenth-century Puritan in her mid-thirties. Her dress resembled a kaftan one might find in an antique shop.

"*Dobroye utro, menya zo—*"

"English is fine."

"Oh," she said, visibly miffed by the correction. "Good morning. My name is Rebecca—never Becca, by the way. I study Russian because I am utterly infatuated by Russian literature. I want to see Saint Petersburg firsthand, see the Hermitage, experience the history. The works of Tolstoy and poetry of Pushkin are so . . . so . . . well . . . these are the very soul of Russia, and I want to feel that. Also, my great-grandmother was from Russia, so I feel connected to the land and its people."

"Great, Rebecca. Thank you." I pointed to the student sitting behind her, a rosy-cheeked young man wearing a hoodie two sizes too big. "How about you?"

"*Zdravstvuitye, menya zo—*"

"English, please."

"Oh yeah," he said. "Should I stand?"

"I don't care."

The kid remained seated. "Name's Ben. I'm ROTC.

Originally from Texas. Did a DNA test that showed I'm two percent Russian. After that, got super into nineteenth-century Russian literature. Amazing how nearly two hundred years later, no writers have been able to capture the soul like those old Russians. I consider them to be the most human of human beings. While I don't think any of us in this room could ever truly understand the Russian soul, I want to give it a what fer."

"You."

A kid wearing baggy shorts and a faded flannel rose from his chair. "Guess I thought it'd be cool to see Europe."

"Europe?"

"Yeah. France, or Russia, something like that,"

"Any reason you chose Russia over France, or something like that?"

He shrugged. I breathed and got stickier.

"Your name?"

"Chris."

"Chris, you're going to do just fine," I said.

The final kid was packaged with watermelon shoulders, muscular calves, and the face of a seven-year-old. "My name is Forrest—two Rs. Zeta Beta Tan! All-state lacrosse champ in high school. I like to have a good time." He glanced around the room, wearing a cocky smile. "Everyone's thinking it, but no one's saying it. Russian women are sexy. Best in the world. The question is, why would you need another reason besides that to want to live there? My buddy coaches lacrosse over there, so I'm guaranteed a spot on the team. Russians are natural Zeta Beta Tans. Bet they go almost as hard as I do."

A sigh escaped me. I'd held this job four years, and I couldn't determine who I found more detestable: Russian soul kids or connoisseurs of Russian females.

Flannel Chris raised his hand.

"Yes?"

"What if I don't like my host family?"

"You haven't even met them yet."

"I know, I'm just saying. What if it turns out I don't like 'em?"

"Are you going in presuming to dislike them?"

Another shrug.

A late entry came through the door. A tall, gangly kid, wearing a green-and-black striped shirt, a red plaid scarf, and square, thick-rimmed glasses. He sat down and, without prompting, stood back up. "*Dobroye utro, menya zovut* Alex. I like Russian, but moreover, I'm a writer."

"Oh?" I said. "What have you written?"

"Nothing yet," the kid replied. "The plan is to write while I'm in Russia. No better place than Russia to soak up inspiration for the soul. The writers who come from there are a testament to that."

"Indeed."

This year's finest. The best the university had to offer to represent the American people in Russia: three Russian soul kids, one sexpat, and one moron.

"So tell me," I said, addressing the group, "what do you think the most difficult part of living in Russia will be? Anyone?"

Stick to the script. That was Valerie's mantra. "Prepare them," she said, "but don't discourage them. Remember, we need this program to expand. Make Russia sound as pleasant and desirable a destination as possible. If students give you Russian soul, lean into it. Describe the rich history of the cuisine. Touch on potential worries, like culture shock and potential faux pas, but do not dwell on them."

How did that one student describe the Russian soul during last year's orientation? "A great sense of humor, thick skin, being in harmony with nature, frankness, fierce loyalty, impossible to comprehend by outsiders."

Um, okay.

"Rebecca," I said. "Can you define for me the Russian soul?"

"It's a riddle wrapped in a mystery inside an enigma." Rebecca—don't call her Becca—flashed a self-satisfied smile. "It's what binds the nation together. It's who and how Russians are. Comprehensible only to those who live there. Um…"

"Everyone got that?" I cleared my throat. "Seeing as none of you answered my earlier question, let me tell you a story that combines the Russian soul and the difficulties of living in Russia. Do any of you know who Paul Thatcher is?"

Blank faces.

"He's an alumnus here," I said. "Graduated a number of years back. He took part in the year-long program in Saint Petersburg. Same time as me. Like many of those who participate in study-abroad programs, he felt compelled to return to Russia. The simplest, most economical way to do this is to become an English teacher. But while his peers were settling in Moscow and Piter, Paul found himself in Volgograd. Some facts about Volgograd: In 2015 it was listed as the most depressing city in all of Russia. The year before, it was awarded with the prize of worst roads in Russia. The locals claim it's the longest city in the world. It's not. A truly splendid and remarkable city."

"Paul was twenty-four when he arrived in the city that once bore the name Stalingrad. We all liked Paul. Mostly for how unremarkable he was. He possessed the most inoffensive face you could imagine. Wore his hair short, simple. No, he was not the most exciting guy in the world, but that's part of what made him so appealing.

"After a year of teaching English in the city, Paul returned home for the summer. The year had been stressful—weeks without running water, not just in his home but the city at large, and more unruly teenagers than anybody should have to deal with. While he also taught adults, Paul's students consisted primarily of teens who gave new meaning to the words *spoiled* and *indifferent*. He spent more time with them than his friends and colleagues, and by the end of the term, Paul was convinced that they, and he, walked away knowing less English than at the beginning. There is a remarkably high turnover rate with English teachers across the globe, but especially in Russia. And especially in Volgograd. Some last less than the full year before calling it quits. Nonetheless, Paul's decision to return to Volgograd after his initial stint was surprising but predictable.

"After landing in the city the first time, Paul had waited almost a week before finding the courage to explore the area and attempt to interact with locals. To small-town Paul, new environments were intimidating, and Volgograd, in particular, being that it was not a hub for expats, like Moscow or Piter, where one can go their entire stay interacting only with other expats. In Volgograd, you either befriended the one or two other English teachers or made nice with the locals.

"This time, as his plane descended and the familiar gray apartment blocks came into view, Paul decided to take the city by storm. He would go looking for fun and cherish the period before work began. He would meet new people and surprise his coworkers, who, when he departed the previous year, had bid him farewell, never presuming he had plans to return.

"His apartment in Volgograd was an insult. The first, mind you, had been far from perfect, but at least it was near the office and located in the city center, close to bars, shops, and cafés. This time around, they had placed him in a building so far from the office as to seem pointed, malicious. The flat itself was cramped, bore a ceiling with an ominous sag, and had a bedroom with a window that didn't close all the way, creating an open invitation for insects in the summer and where, in the winter, Paul would be unable to escape the region's brutal, icy winds."

The coffee on my shirt was drying, leaving behind a sticky residue.

"Despite his disappointment, Paul set down his bags and made himself presentable. He brushed his teeth, combed his hair, put on a gray Oxford shirt, then pulled on a navy blue cardigan, from Benetton, a purchase he was especially proud of . . ."

~~~

Paul hurried down the hallway and into the stairwell, both enclosed by drab green walls and lighted by widely spaced bare bulbs—most of them burned out. He nearly tripped on the last two steps before bounding out onto the sidewalk, where he was greeted by a woman's screams, thanks to a dozen or so large dogs who were circling her as she tried to enter the building. Each time she made an attempt, one of the dogs would break the circle and lunge at her feet. Paul thought he recognized one of them—short hair, white, with black around its eyes—as one that used to follow him home at night, begging for shawarma. While not positive, they were likely the same dogs that used to chase cyclists. His stomach rumbled, but he decided it wasn't of any concern. Going back upstairs in this sweat-inducing
~~~

heat wasn't worth the effort. Also not worth the effort was waiting for the metro. Volgograd's metro wasn't so much a metro as a tram that sometimes went underground. Unlike its famous Moscow counterpart, it wasn't the pride of the country nor punctual. By the time it would take to wait for it, he'd be at his destination on foot. That destination was the office. He was excited to surprise his coworkers with his return. When he'd left the previous year, they gave him their farewells, convinced he'd want to stay as far away from this city as possible.

He passed by the shopping center referred to by the locals as Torgushka, and was pleased to see the local youth working hard at the ancient Volgograd tradition of standing in front of a building but never entering it nor moving from their spot. A word he ensured his previous year's students never forgot. One simple word that summed up the essence of Russians and what they do more effectively than any poet, writer, or member of the intelligentsia ever could.

"Paul, remind me please, what is the word you taught us last year?"

"Sergey?" Paul turned to see a familiar face.

Sergey was as tall as he was thin, kept his hair short, and dressed with incredible style. A style one couldn't really put a time or place to. Think equal parts Kanye West and Eddie Murphy *Raw*. Paul liked and feared him and wasn't convinced he wasn't a member of the FSB.

"Hello Paul. Remember last year you told us a word that Russians do?" Sergey said, sauntering up to Paul. "You know, whenever you asked what we did at the weekend and we told you we 'walked with friends' and you didn't know what that meant, so you tell us it was 'hanging out.' But then you say that not right because hanging out means doing something, and

Russians don't do anything. They just stand in front of place and do nothing. What is word?"

"Loitering."

"Yes!" A wide smile broke across Sergey's face. "Loitering. Thank you. This is very useful word."

"What are you doing in this part of town, Sergey?"

"Getting rich, Paul. Getting rich." He pulled out his iPhone and brought up his notepad. "And here, look at this."

On the screen in front of Paul was a list:

Nastya

Nastya +1

Anya

Masha +1

Masha +2

Katya +1

On and on it went. All four names for Russian women represented with some variation of "Anya" or "Anka."

Paul scrolled through at least a hundred before stopping. "What am I looking at here?"

"Every girl I ever fuck. What do the pluses mean?"

"I was just getting to that. Well?"

"Plus one means blow job included," Sergey said. "Plus two is threesome."

Paul handed back the phone. "You and two women?"

"No. One woman with me and friend."

"So you don't prefer a threesome with two women?"

"No," he said. "Two men. When you with friend, much more funnier."

"Sergey," Paul said, "remember when I explained the difference between fun and funny? If you mean *exciting*, the word is *fun*. If you mean you *laughed*, the word is *funny*."

"*Da*," Sergey said.

"Okay."

"But, Paul, I tell you, threesome with friend and one girl is better. When you get tired or bored, your friend can take over, while you loiter in the back and watch."

"I understand." Paul started away.

"Be careful today, dude," Sergey called after him. "Is national holiday. Many crazy gopniks and nationalists out. Drunk. Don't let them hear you speak English. Oh, I ask one more question?"

Paul stopped and turned. "Of course."

"Is true Americans think they won World War the Second?"

Paul waved him off and continued down the street.

Getting to the office required crossing a bridge that connected Paul's neighborhood to the city center. The bridge stretched and stretched, seeming never to end, but it wasn't the longest bridge in the city. That honor had been given to the one locals claimed was the longest in all of Europe. It wasn't.

Paul walked the bridge, on either side of which were barren, dried-up ponds, tumbleweeds, and empty bottles of Baltika #9. About halfway across, Paul spotted a couple of guys he recognized walking in the opposite direction. Both were American English teachers from a rival school in another part of town. As foreigners tend to do, the two congregated regularly, often at the same bars and cafés. Paul never made much effort to interact with them. Though not quite sexpats, they were fuckboys—an attitude that made up almost the entire essence of their characters. John Pindos, the shorter and dumpier of the two, was from somewhere in New England and fancied himself an intellectual. Michael—Paul couldn't recall his last name—at six feet two, towered over his partner in crime and wore a perpetually smug expression. He was a certified cicerone and never let Paul or anyone else forget it. Had even stated that his training, in beer, rivaled that of the Navy SEALs.

Not wishing to draw their attention, Paul kept his head down as they passed.

As the trek across the bridge stretched on, a matter materialized that could very well threaten Paul's day: two khaki-wearing Mormon youths, sporting the standard crisp white shirts. The very same Mormons he had encountered the previous year, on this very same bridge. Unless he was willing to jump over the side, Paul was on a collision course with the word of Joseph Smith. He knew from experience that his usual bag of tricks wouldn't work on these two. While it was not in Paul's nature to reject people, having no intention of converting, he had tried initially to respond to the missionaries in Russian.

They had replied in perfect Mormon-accented Russian.

Upon realization that Paul was, in fact, American, the boys had exchanged a glance, their eyes lighting up with hope. Forty-five minutes later, when Paul finally summoned the courage to bid the two farewell, he ended up promising to keep in touch. He had not. Paul had to give them credit for their craftiness and endurance, having recognized the bridge as the perfect location to do their work. Where death was the only escape.

Their beaming smiles indicated their recognition of Paul, who did not know how to smile and, hence, had never been comfortable appearing in photos. Not yet willing to plummet to his demise, and understanding that merely rushing past the pair would be a fruitless effort—Mormon missionaries were notoriously fast runners—Paul did the only thing he could do: dashed through the middle of their two-bodied wall, splitting them apart, and then ran like hell. Classic divide and conquer.

Sweat was forming a shallow pool beneath his arms when he finally came to a stop. After several seconds, he caught his breath and looked back. The bridge was clear. His stomach twisted and creaked. He wiped sweat from his brow and reassured himself that his stomach troubles were nothing to worry about.

The sweltering air, now alive with insects, had thickened. Like dogs who had learned to navigate the metro system moving in proud pacts, area gnats had learned to penetrate the closed mouths, nostrils, eyes, and ears of anyone who dared walk outside in warm weather. Like most animals here, the Russian gnat was more aggressive and bloodthirsty than their American counterparts. Joined occasionally by mosquitos and the odd beetle, thick clouds of gnats continued to plague Paul as he stepped off the bridge and made his way toward the city center.

Foot traffic, as usual, was heavy. Paul traversed wide boulevards with care, trying to avoid Russians desperate, it seemed, to walk into him. He was finally picking up speed when a young Russian male stopped abruptly in front of him and bent down to tie his shoe.

Paul tripped over the kid and landed hard on his right knee.

Two Russians then proceeded to trip over Paul.

The youth, satisfied with his efforts, straightened and went on his way.

As Paul sat on the pavement, knee covered in blood, the two Russians began shouting abuse. With a groan, Paul pushed to his feet and took off at a jog. He crossed the street and hopped onto a less-congested, narrow walkway lined with trees. He was walking along, enjoying the bits of shade, when another Russian, older this time, bent down in the middle of the footpath to tie his shoe.

Paul tripped over him, managing to save his good knee by once again landing on the injured one. He remained on the ground for a time as gnats tore at his flesh.

"What a terrible country," he muttered.

"Paul?"

A female voice, familiar yet impossible.

Paul stood, beholding the most beautiful girl in all of Volgograd.

~~~

"Was she a smoke show?" Forrest asked.

"A what?"

"A smoke show."

"I have no idea what that is."

"You know, a babe. A fine specimen."

"Well, she was enough of a *babe*, as you say, to temporarily paralyze Paul."

"Yeah, but what kind of Russian babe was she?"

Forrest's smarmy smile made my skin crawl.

"Kind?"

"Look, bro," Forrest said, "there are different genres of Russian broads. Was she a blond ice queen? A brunette with
~~~

big pouty lips? A Moscow type with a big fur coat and high heels? Maybe she was a Russian Jew? That's a category all its own—different from Russian and different from regular Jew. And then there's my favorite: the peasant look."

"Peasant look?"

"Yeah," he said. "Think like, stupidly big eyes, far apart. Flat, round face. Simple looking, like she should be milking a cow in some field in Siberia." He chuckled. "Know how you find out if a chick is from Siberia?"

"No," I said. "Why don't you educate us?"

"Shave her head bald. If she looks like an alien, she's Siberian."

~~~

How did she know my name?

Paul, on the other hand, was very much aware of hers. Olga.

She was taller than he. If Volgograd couldn't claim the longest bridge in Europe, Olga, at least, could claim the longest legs in Volgograd. She wore an outfit of all-white, making her look like an angel. Her hair, worn long, was dark and wavy.

Even while being assaulted by gnats, Olga managed to retain her poise.

During his first stint in the city, Paul would wait in the corridor every evening after his six o'clock lesson, hoping to catch a glimpse of her, but he never dared approach. Mostly because he couldn't think of anything to say. She was Ryan's student. And while there were attractive female students in Paul's class, none left him thunderstruck as Olga had.

"What are you doing here?" she asked.

In contrast to the typical, stunted Volgograd variety,
~~~

Olga's English was quite good.

Well, it was okay. Actually, it wasn't great.

"I'm teaching again." Even in this stifling heat, he could smell her enticing perfume.

"That is so great." She smiled, tilting her head. "Most American teachers leave after one year. So great that you stay."

"Yeah?"

"It is pity, though. I will not attend your school on this year."

Paul frowned. "A pity, indeed."

"I always hear how fun were your classes," she said. "I wanted you to be my teacher. Well, goodbye, Paul."

Olga started away, then turned back. "Hey, Paul," she said. "Tonight we with friends are walking. Some clubs, listen some music. You will come?"

Paul nodded. "You know, I think I will."

Paul had dreamed of getting Olga's phone number, but had never let himself believe it could actually happen. Now here she was giving it to Paul, without him even having to ask. His sore knee no longer mattered. Nor did the insects feasting on his flesh.

He took off toward the office, his optimism and confidence renewed.

What had he done right to make this happen? While he'd never admit it—especially not to any Russians—Paul was a young American male and was, like most, as smitten with the women of Russia as anyone else.

He looked down at his mobile. Even the digits of her phone number were sexy.

"What a fantastic country," he said, then tripped over a

Russian tying his shoes. This time he broke his fall with both knees.

Paul's place of employment was located in one of the city's tallest buildings on one of the city's most prominent streets. Across from the building was a supermarket where Paul had encountered many a stressful situation trying to explain to the women behind the counter which prepackaged salad he would like to purchase. Despite his history of experiencing torture at both locations, while presently strolling the neighborhood, Paul was overcome by nostalgia.

He had the attention of a beautiful girl. He could set aside his pain. More difficult to set aside was his shirt, which by now was soaked with sweat. As he had learned to do during his first tenure here, Paul found a public bathroom, ran the shirt under the faucet, using a generous amount of soap at the underarms, and held it under the hand dryer.

Once back out on the sunny sidewalk, Paul's attitude brightened again.

As he stood in front of the supermarket, readying himself to cross the street, he spotted a familiar face coming his way.

How unexpected, he thought. Sasha was a former student and a girl newly nineteen.

~~~

"Why is that important?" Rebecca asked.

"What's that?"

"Why did you mention that she recently turned nineteen?"

"I can see why including that detail might seem odd," I conceded. "I include it here only because when people hear
~~~

stories about teachers being attracted to their students, they tend to assume things. I feel it's important to stress that the students, in this case, were adults."

"Still seems inappropriate," Rebecca shot back. "Teachers hitting on their students."

"I never stated that Paul hit on her."

~~~

Like most straight American men teaching English in Volgograd, Paul embraced the attention of female ADULT students. But, though Paul found Sasha attractive, he had never pursued her. At least, not in that way. He and Sasha had gone out several times, but only as friends. Quite genuinely, in fact, Paul enjoyed their friendship.

After he returned to the States, Paul received a text message from Sasha:

I'm sorry, Paul, but we can
no longer correspond with
one another. My boyfriend,
Stas, does not like how much
time I spend talking to you.

A pity, Paul had thought at the time. But he understood. The Russian male, by nature, was a jealous creature.

Paul hadn't thought about Sasha in months, and it did not occur to him that Stas, by this time, would still be having any thoughts about him. So, when Sasha, with Stas in tow, approached, Paul flashed a broad grin, unconcerned that such a greeting might constitute an insult.

He was wrong.
~~~

Stas stepped between Sasha and Paul. "Why you coming on to my woman?"

Paul's smile turned to a frown. "What? I—"

"Asshole!" Stas said. "Amerikos!"

Paul, growing nervous, turned to Sasha with an apologetic shrug.

"Don't look at her!"

"I wasn't looking, I—"

"You come back here for her?" Stas said, his voice growing ever louder. "You have some fucking nerve."

"But nothing ever—"

"Don't try to lie. I read your messages. She show me."

"Wait," Paul said. "You can read English?"

Stas's eyes narrowed on Paul. "Arrogant, piece-of-shit American."

"Nothing happened between Sasha and me. She's your woman. I'm not here for her. I'm here to work and see my friends."

"I not buy it," Stas said. "We settle this."

"There's nothing to settle. I'm an adult. I don't fight."

"You saying I not an adult?"

"There's no winning with you, is there?" Paul said, his heart hammering in his chest. "This is going nowhere. Good day to you."

Paul walked off.

That wasn't so hard, he thought. Just one foot in front of the other. While shaken by the incident, Paul was relieved to have gotten away relatively easily. Too often, he had heard stories from his American peers, unfortunate souls who had found themselves in the company of gopniks, or worse.

He passed the café he'd buy his morning coffee from when suddenly he saw stars. There was no pain. Pain would come later. It hadn't occurred to Paul that he had been punched in the back of the neck. He was now being repeatedly struck in the side of the head, though, miraculously, he remained on his feet. He never thought to put up his hands in defense. Never thought to put up a fight at all. In fairness to Paul, he wasn't thinking of anything at all. There were only stars buzzing around him. Constellations that formed and dissipated with each consecutive punch.

Soon everything went hazy, and Paul desired only to sleep.

Pedestrians passed by, paying little mind to the incident. Of far more interest were the two packs of wild dogs warring each other from either side of the street. When neither pack seemed inclined to back down, the pack on the opposite side charged, running into traffic, with several cars swerving to avoid hitting the animals.

The two packs collided in front of Paul's office building—all except one dog that strayed from the action to chase down a woman carrying groceries away from the supermarket. Few cared about what was happening to Paul, save for two bystanders, Russians, who reluctantly intervened and managed to throw off the vengeful Stas.

Sasha walked off with her victorious boyfriend, the two of them, apparently, declining English lessons for the day. Paul, his vision blurred, never saw whether Sasha showed any remorse.

His saviors were two men around his age.

"You all right?" one of them asked.

"Fine. I'm fine." Though Paul wasn't so sure, he didn't care to become a stranger's burden.

"No, you're not. You need to go to the hospital immediately," said the second.

"Truly, I'm fine. There's no need for any of that,"

"Idiot," said the first, "You've been struck in the head multiple times, and you're covered in blood,"

"In blood?" Paul repeated.

Looking down, he found his gray shirt was three-fourths covered in fresh, dark red blood.

"Oh," said Paul, "I can just wash it off,"

"You can't wash off a torn ear," said the first.

"A torn ear?"

His hand reached for his right ear, but it was slapped away by the first rescuer. The two men looked horrified.

"Your ear is like this," said the first, tearing an imaginary piece of paper in half. Paul reached for his ear once more to check if what he believed they meant is what they actually meant. Once more they reacted in horror and prevented him from touching his ear that had been torn in two as easily as tissue paper. Blood continued to shoot onto his shirt, his pants, and the ground below. One of the men returned with a handful of paper towels and instructed Paul to gently wrap them around his pieces of ear and apply pressure.

"Will you find your way to the hospital?" the first asked.

Paul gave a thumbs up.

~~~

"Did he ever make it to the hospital?" Chris asked.

"He did."

"How?"
~~~

“Does it matter?”

“Of course it matters,” Rebecca said. “Did he get in a cab? Did someone from his office drive him? Did he crawl there?”

“He just got there. Do we really need to know how? I cleared my throat. “So, Russian hospitals look the same as every other building in Russia: dull green walls, dark hallways, flickering lights, random holes in walls and floors, and ceilings ready to cave in at the slightest provocation. After finding his way to one of the hospital’s dilapidated waiting areas, Paul planted himself down between two Adidas-clad gopniks.”

“What’s a gopnik?” Chris asked. “You keep mentioning it.”

“Think if Adidas and cigarettes merged into one being and became sentient.”

“What?”

~~~

The two gopniks sitting on either side of Paul had massive swellings where their eyes ought to have been. A third gopnik with his leg in a cast sat directly across from Paul. Farther down the long, narrow waiting room sat several women who had been terrorized by a pack of stray dogs.

Pain began to register in Paul’s head, making his stomach turn. He got up from the bench to search for a toilet.

“Paul!” a fat nurse shouted. “You’re bleeding all over the floor!”

All three gopniks turned at the sound of the foreign name and watched as Paul made his way back.

He shot an apologetic glance toward the nurse as she approached, realizing that “fat” wasn’t quite the right word to describe her.
~~~

"Sit!" she barked.

Paul sat on the slab.

"Look at you." She roughly dabbed at his ear with a piece of gauze. "Such a mess."

"I'm sorry."

"Sorry, he says." A set of bloated cheeks threatened to engulf her shallow, sunken face. "Sorry won't clean up this floor."

A younger, nicer-looking medical professional—nurse, doctor, or other, Paul couldn't be sure—arrived on the scene and sewed Paul's ear back into place. "Before I let you go," he said, "I'll need some details about your injury for our files."

Paul told the tale, emphasizing the point—not that it mattered for the purpose of his medical file—that he had not, in fact, come to Volgograd for nineteen-year-old Sasha.

"Protocol dictates we report this to the police," the young man said.

"Please don't," Paul said.

"We must."

"But I don't want to involve the police."

"I see." The guy nodded knowingly. "Well, then, let me ask you this." He tapped the report with his pen. "Are you sure this is your official statement?"

After a beat, Paul caught on. "I slipped and fell down the stairs?"

"If you say so."

With his ear freshly stitched up, Paul was free to go. Not so fresh was his shirt, more brown than red now that the blood had dried. They sent him away with pain meds, explicitly stating not to mix the tablets with alcohol.

~~~

No longer caring about the element of surprise, Paul sent a text to his colleague, Tyler, who had never said no to a drink in his life. Tyler didn't question what Paul was doing back in Volgograd and readily agreed to meet him. Paul stared down at his phone. Was it really almost ten o'clock? The realization made his head hurt.

Tyler was one of the few American teachers Paul could stand. While he was often too loud and excitable for Paul's liking, he wasn't a sexpat, gave two shits about the Russian soul, and had actually bothered to learn the language. He liked to drink, though this hardly made up the whole of his personality.

Rather than meet somewhere Paul liked, Tyler inexplicably suggested one of the tackiest spots in the city. Black Dog was interchangeable with many of Volgograd's other bars, in that the name was a combination of a color and an animal. The bulk of its clientele were sleazy foreigners—more Turks than Americans, in this case—looking to hook up with trashy local women seeking foreigners willing to spend big on them, their friends, and their boyfriends.

When the weather was agreeable, they opened the terrace, so people could drink, puke, and urinate outside as well as in. It was less than a proper terrace, however, and the drinking and general rottenness more often than not tended to spill into the streets and other establishments. The entire area smelled perpetually of piss, as well as chemicals designed to hide the smell of piss.

Inside, like most comparable Russian establishments, one found a writhing, breathing mass five to ten times the reasonable capacity. A fire hazard, to be sure.
~~~

To Paul's horror, Tyler texted that he was inside.

To Paul's surprise, Tyler had managed to score a table on the top floor.

Getting to said table, however, was problematic, at best. The narrow hallway leading up allowed comfortable passage for one body at a time. Despite this, Paul entered the area to find an excess of patrons moving in both directions at once. He pushed his way through, holding his breath against a sea of drunken sweat, as well as cigarette smoke that irritated his eyes and nostrils.

At the table, Tyler sat, looking half-asleep, cigarette hanging from his lips. Paul didn't know if Tyler had smoked before coming to Russia, but he certainly smoked his share now. Sitting beside Tyler was an attractive young woman, and to Paul, this made no sense. The face was familiar; it was Anna, their receptionist. Not counting himself, nearly every American guy working at the school had asked her out, or at least had made a lame attempt to get her out for drinks. She had declined every single invitation.

Yet here she was with Tyler.

Tyler, as it happened, was uninterested, as well as unsurprised, by Paul's stitches and his bloodied shirt. Paul, for his part, was not offended. In fact, he felt a sense of relief to find some normalcy, care of Tyler, in the day.

The beer was terrible—rancid and watered down, as if the kegs hadn't been cleaned since Gorbachev, and the water had been drawn from the downstairs urinals. As if someone had drunk the urinal beer and vomited it back into the plastic cup to serve to customers.

While the steady flow of alcohol and meds dimmed Paul's pain, the pounding bass from the sound system thrummed uncomfortably in Paul's injured ear. For twenty minutes now, Tyler had been talking about the book he was writing—on the Russian soul—the details of which Paul was finding progressively more difficult to follow. Soon the euphoria of seeing an old friend and forgetting the day's events gave way to a gurgling in Paul's stomach.

~~~

"Sorry to interrupt," Alex said, "but what was included in Tyler's book?"

"I couldn't tell you."

"I just ask because I'm also writing a book on the Russian soul, and I don't want to step on any toes."

"Well, likely you'll reach similar conclusions."

Forrest leaned into Alex and whispered, "I'll bet that Anna's a peasant."

~~~

Paul had to take a shit. He had passed the threshold, when holding it was no longer an option. It was half past ten. The metro was open until eleven. The final train departed five minutes later. It was only one stop from here to his apartment, but, even so, holding it would be tough. Doable, if necessary, but tough. "I think I'm going to get going, guys," he said.

Tyler gestured he hadn't heard over the hard bass.

"I'm going to get going!"

"Can you wait two minutes?" Anna flashed a charming smile.

"Why?"

The two of them stood.

"I'm going to go with her to the bathroom," Tyler said.

"Could you watch our stuff? Back in two minutes."

"Yeah, okay. But please don't take long. I really need to get going."

As the couple hurried off, leaving two backpacks behind, the rumbling in Paul's stomach began to challenge the bass-heavy music for dominance. Paul eyed the crowd. Somehow even more people had managed to squeeze inside the place. He recalled with unease an incident in which a Moscow club had burned to the ground, killing hundreds who had no way out.

He noted a few women present, but the vast majority were young men, who seemingly had no problem dancing their hearts out to the pulsating Eurodance without a partner.

Paul wished he could be so carefree.

He checked his phone. Quarter to eleven. "Back in two minutes," he muttered.

When another two minutes had passed, Paul grabbed their heavy bags and made his way downstairs. If upstairs felt oppressive with the number of bodies, downstairs were levels four through seven of Dante's *Inferno*. A thick sea of wriggling arms, bobbing heads, and sweat. To his annoyance, he spotted Tyler and Anna on the dance floor, arms and lips tightly wrapped around each other.

Paul wasn't about to wade into the ocean of bodies.

He glanced at the line for the bathroom, by his count about a dozen people long. He avoided public bathrooms in Russia whenever he could. If he joined the queue now, he would most certainly miss his train. He hurried back upstairs, left his friends' bags with the bartender, and made haste to the metro, arriving with eight minutes to spare.

With the worst of this disastrous day, and night, behind

him, Paul looked forward to an uneventful train ride, followed by a well-deserved sleep. While the speed in getting there was necessary, it had added pressure to his bowels, so once the metro entrance was in sight, he slowed, taking calm, calculated steps. He was in arm's reach of the entry door when he heard a gruff, authoritative voice.

"*Molodoy chelovek!*"

Paul stopped and turned, coming face-to-face with a police officer—thirtyish, Uzbek by the looks of him, and without an ounce of humor on his face.

What would improve his odds, Paul wondered? Speaking Russian or pretending not to speak Russian? After weighing the options and conceding that he had never been a good liar, Paul responded. "*Dobriy vecher.*"

"Are you drunk?"

"I am not drunk."

The cop studied his face with a skeptical eye. "Your passport. Hand it over."

This wasn't as easy as it sounded. Whereas many of his American peers welcomed the attention being a foreigner in Russia brought them, Paul dreaded it. He didn't look Russian, necessarily, but as long as he kept his mouth shut and his head down, he could usually get through day-to-day life without much hassle.

Until he was asked to show his passport.

Whether it was in line at the local *produkty* or getting onto a train, the handing over, and subsequential opening, of that little blue booklet brought unwanted attention. He found the back-and-forth eyeing of the photo, against Paul in the flesh, particularly distressing.

Though many of his compatriots had, from time to time, lost their passports in nefarious places, Paul's rarely left his right front pants pocket. As a result, sweat and the elements had nearly erased the lettering on the front cover.

"*Amerikanets, chto li?*"

American or something? Rhetorical and meant to be an insult. The officer was baiting him.

Paul nodded.

"Grisha!" barked the officer. "Get over here!"

Grisha was three times the size of the central Asian cop and possessed a gargantuan head—the biggest Paul had ever seen. The cop showed the passport to Grisha, who stared Paul down as if examining a new species. As time wore on, Paul's passport passed through the hands of eight different officers (all looking like Grisha in different stages of his life) until, once again, it was only Paul and the Uzbek cop.

"Where are you headed?" the cop asked.

"Home. Trying to catch the metro before it closes."

"Why did you come to Russia?"

"To teach English."

"Mm. Who won the Second World War?"

"The Soviet Union."

"But in your America, you think you won, don't you? Why do Americans think this?"

Paul shrugged.

"You like it here?"

"Yes, I like it here."

"But you like America more than Russia. It's better there, yes?"

"They are both good, in different ways."

The officer slapped Paul's passport against his left palm, then flipped it open. "I stopped you because you look intoxicated," he said. "Russian Federation law dictates it is illegal to wander the streets while drunk."

"I'm not drunk," Paul said, his head still swimming from the beer and pills. "That's the truth."

"I have eight years' experience. I know drunk when I see it. Show me what's in your pockets."

Paul removed his wallet, a pen, and some loose change. The cop gestured for the wallet and opened it, removing five 100-ruble banknotes. He counted them several times and handed the wallet back to Paul. He held on to the banknotes.

Paul waited, expecting something to happen or for the cop to say something. Neither came. Paul took one step backward, then another. The cop didn't react. Paul then made a run for the metro and pushed through the heavy doors. It was 10:58. He continued on to the old woman working in the small cubicle and gave her his change.

She pushed it back.

"What?" he asked.

"Are you stupid? Twenty rubles."

He had handed her fifteen. The fare must have gone up since he was here last. He searched his pockets and found only three more.

"Please," he begged.

"Twenty!"

Fuck! He dashed to the ATM—a gamble in and of itself as the metro machines were notorious for swallowing cards or refusing to give cash. He tried to withdraw fifty, the smallest amount available, but the lowest the machine was offering was five hundred. *Fuck!*

He withdrew the five hundred and ran back to the old woman.

"What do I do with this?" she asked.

"One ticket," he said.

"I cannot break this. I need something smaller."

"Please, just give me one ticket."

"Bring me something smaller! Next!"

A middled-aged woman tried to shove past Paul.

"Let me get two tickets then," he said.

"The bill is still too big."

"Five tickets!" Paul said.

With a roll of her eyes, the old woman accepted the bill, handing over five tickets. Paul rushed to the turnstile and slipped the ticket into the slot. It spat it back out. He tried again. Same result. The same thing happened at the second turnstile.

Again, he returned to the woman at the window. "It won't accept my ticket. Can you open the gates?"

"It's after eleven," she explained. "The metro is closed."

Paul's temper flared. "Why would you sell me the tickets when you knew it was closed?"

"You have no etiquette!" she huffed.

As much as Paul would have liked to stay and discuss the finer points of common courtesy, the unforeseen delays had threatened serious damage to his intestines. He would never make it across the bridge on foot. He ran out of the metro, past the Uzbek cop, who was currently harassing another unfortunate youth, and ran back to Black Dog, where the number of sweaty patrons had grown tenfold, and Tyler's tongue was now deep inside Anna's mouth. When he joined the queue at the toilets, four people were in line ahead of him.

When finally the young woman directly in front of Paul entered the restroom, he breathed an advanced, though tentative, sigh of relief.

Ten minutes passed, and his leg began to twitch.

Another few minutes and his body began to shake.

Dare he risk leaving, attempt crossing the bridge to shit at home?

He got a text.

> *Paul! Where are you? We are at White Horse! Come! We are celebrating my friend Tanya's happy birthday))). ~Olga.*

In all the day's "excitement," Paul had completely forgotten about Olga. As much as he liked her, after taking care of business, he wanted only to go home and to bed. He stared at the still-closed restroom door and shifted his weight.

Olga sent a follow-up. A photo of herself with three other young women. All brunette. All gorgeous. He recognized one of them as Mila—an acquaintance from the previous year. If Olga was the most beautiful woman Paul had ever seen, Mila was the sexiest—too sexy to be conceived as real.

Finally the door to the toilet opened and the girl walked out.

Thank God!

What greeted him was a horror the likes of which the

city hadn't seen since 1943, when the Germans were involved.

A thick cloud of digested and semi-digested Russian food engulfed Paul before he was even over the threshold—an odor so pungent it could be tasted. Paul's mind flashed back to his time as an exchange student when he could barely stomach the food prepared by his host mother. After weeks of politely gagging it down, Paul began stashing the worst bits in small, plastic bags, which he would tuck away in his backpack, and then throw away at school. Every now and again, he would forget a bag, buried deep in his pack, only to remember it weeks later when the smell of spoiled pickles and rotten eggs, mixed with kasha, seeped through the bag. In one incident, while still on campus, the forgotten bag had somehow torn open, producing a stench so horrendous it caused him to projectile vomit outside his classroom door.

Paul surveyed his current surroundings.

Where the puke ended and the shit began was anyone's guess. Putrid bits of kasha, mayonnaise, and kholodets seemed to have climbed out of the toilet bowl, spread onto the rim, and dripped onto the floor, meeting there what appeared to be a pile of puke. Was it all from one person? Did that person shit so hard they caused themselves to puke? Paul lifted and inspected his shoes, now rimmed with sludge.

He considered dropping his trousers, bending forward, and, while standing, shitting in the direction of the toilet. It occurred to him then that he could shit anywhere in this room. What difference, really, would it make?

Adding insult to injury, there was no toilet paper or paper towels to be found.

Sadly, this was typical of public restrooms in Russia, and the reason Paul went out of his way, whenever possible, to avoid them. He walked out of the bathroom and out of Black Dog. Once back on the sidewalk, Paul drew a breath of fresh, mosquito-infested air, momentarily easing his distress.

Momentarily.

Before him, the streets were overrun with high-heeled, short-skirted, made-up women, patrolling the uneven pavement like baby giraffes. In Russia, the real drinking and partying didn't start for another two hours, so Paul found it peculiar, this high level of early activity.

His phone map indicated White Horse at only eight minutes away on foot, while walking back to his place would be a twenty-five minute affair.

He could survive eight minutes. Twenty-five he wasn't so sure.

He passed by Kvartal. Monday through Friday evening, Kvartal was nothing more than a produkty—a quickie mart. Three aisles, nothing remarkable. On Friday evenings after nine thirty, it became a hub of all Caucasian activity. Lads from Ingushetia and Chechnya, and mostly Dagestan, pulled up in their BMWs and Lada sedans, parked in front, and blasted their Kavkaz Sila themed hip-hop and lezginka music. One did not enter this territory if not prepared to meet whatever challenge the Caucasians proposed.

The small café on the other side of Kvartal was sure to have a toilet. There was no reason to believe it did not. En route, Paul, now desperate to evacuate his bowels, walked unwittingly into the sights of Tamerlan the Mighty, who was admiring his recently acquired 1998 BMW.

By the time Paul realized his error, it was too late.

"Ey!" Despite standing at a mere five foot six, Tamerlan

the Mighty possessed the presence and confidence of a man eight foot six. "Got a problem?" He moved in front of Paul, nearly stepping on his toes, and then his eyes narrowed as if penetrating Paul's clothing and skin, as if seeing through to his jittering heart.

Paul, keeping his head down, attempted to walk around the diminutive giant. After the earlier instance with the law enforcer, Paul decided he no longer knew any Russian.

"Ey!"

The second call from the Mighty sent his twelve-man task force into action, surrounding Paul.

~~~

"What is this?" Chris asked.

"What?"

"I don't follow what's happening."

"Where did I lose you?"

"You keep saying that these dudes are Caucasian. I mean, we're talking about Europe, right? Isn't most everyone Caucasian?"

"Let's back up a minute. Caucasian, in the Russian context, doesn't mean a white person. The terms aren't interchangeable there. Rather, it refers to someone from the Caucasus Mountains. Are any of you familiar with the Caucasus?"

No response.

"It's a region in southern Russia. I'm sure some of you at least have heard of the Chechen conflicts. The Caucasus is where those took place. Many Russians carry negative feelings and stereotypes toward Caucasians, who have their own
~~~

culture—languages, customs, religions. To confuse matters further, Caucasians are often darker skinned than Russians, and some Russians go so far as to refer to them as black. Kind of wild, huh? Black Caucasians?"

"I don't find it *wild* at all," Rebecca said. "I find it highly offensive."

"It's meant to be offensive."

"And that makes it okay?"

I sighed inwardly. "Anyway..."

~~~

"You deaf, you goat?" said the Caucasian to Paul's right.

"Actually, yes," Paul replied. "A little bit."

"What you say?" This, from the Mighty himself.

"What's that?" Paul's hand moved to his injured ear.

"Give us one thousand rubles."

"I don't have a thousand rubles."

"Look, *bratan*." The Mighty crossed his arms. "I do not care what you don't have. Give to me what I want."

"I have nothing," Paul said. "Look." Paul showed them his empty pockets and wallet.

"You know," the Mighty said. "You're a real jerk. Just a thousand rubles is all I need. So me and my brothers here can screw some sluts. You really don't have one thousand rubles?"

"I don't," The medication and the booze were wearing off, and Paul's head began to ache. "I'm sorry."

"Where are you from?" the Mighty asked.

At this question, Paul had multiple choices. The truth, he knew, could prompt an onslaught of uncomfortable questions
~~~

he wasn't so eager to answer. He could say Australia, but realizing they might have a working knowledge of the land down under he could not fake, Paul's best bet was probably New Zealand.

"I'm from America."

Silence as the Mighty and his boys took in this information. Even the blasting music from their car stereos seemed to pause on his command.

"Do you speak English?" the Mighty asked.

"Of course."

"Please bro," Tamerlan switched to English. "Bro, you must to help me in English. I want very much go to the America. My dream. My brother there now lives in the Los Angeles and work in central casting. He in episodes *NCIS: Los Angeles* and *Nurse Jackie*. You watch? I try get visa. They say no me. They ask I am terrorist. I want see brother. You help me better my English and help me get visa and help me my brother,"

"I will help you," said Paul.

"This is good. Tell me please, in the America, are there many the Jews?"

"Uh, I don't know. Kind of?"

Tamerlan sighed and shook his head. The weight of all the world's burdens moved back and forth.

"In Russia same problem. Jew is very cunning. Always make scheme. But I am Kavkaz. I crush Jew if he schemes to me. Tell me, what is your name?"

"Paul."

"Paul, are you the Jew?"

"No, I am not the Jew."

"Paul, I not racist. I very tolerant. If you Jew and I from Kavkaz and you respect me, we drink together as brothers. Drink with me."

He pulled a bottle out of his jacket pocket. Paul had initially taken the green-striped tracksuit for Adidas, when, in fact, he noted, upon closer inspection, the label spelled *Abibas*. Tamerlan the Mighty and all his boys, as it happened, wore Abibas. Paul took a swig of the warm vodka, and then another as the Mighty pushed the bottle back toward Paul's mouth.

"You have girlfriend?" he asked.

Paul shook his head.

"If you find thousand rubles for me and three thousand for you, we will screw some sluts with you, brother."

Paul gazed in the direction of the café, trying to figure a polite way to flee. But each time an opportune moment presented itself, the Mighty pulled him close with another question.

"*Kavkaz sila!*" yelled one of the brothers.

"Kavkaz sila!" the rest returned in unison.

"Tamerlan sila!"

From the corner of his eye, Paul spotted a Russian youth making the same mistake he had just minutes ago.

"Hey, bratan," said Tamerlan the Mighty, stepping in the kid's path. "Say Tamerlan sila." He threw a glass bottle at the kid's feet.

"Tamerlan sila?" the kid said. "What the hell?"

The Mighty narrowed his eyes. "You motherfucker."

Before the young Russian could feel the power of the Mighty's wrath, a man, burly and with a distinct air of confidence, arrived on the scene. Burly or not, Paul thought the man foolish for approaching the gang as he did. Behind him came a cameraman, along with a dozen or so healthy young lads.

"Good evening," said the head of the crew.

"What the fuck?"

Before the Mighty received his answer, a second cameraman appeared from some nearby bushes. Paul, just as confused as his new Caucasian friends, faltered, then regained his footing.

A third cameraman, tying his shoes, was crouched closer to the café.

"What the hell is with the cameras?" the Mighty asked.

"Is this your alcohol?" The head of the crew gestured to several full and half-full vodka and Baltika Devyatka bottles in the area.

"I say, what is this?" The Mighty set his hands on his hips. "Who are you? Get your cameras out of my face."

Two of the cameramen were only inches away from Tamerlan, collecting his breath on their lenses.

"By law of the Russian Federation," the first man said, "it is illegal to drink in public spaces. Children walk these streets and parks. Families. Is this the image we should be showing the youth and future of this country?"

The Mighty came inches from the man's face. "Who the fuck do you think you are?"

"Don't curse," the man said. "It's unbecoming."

"Fuck you. I am Tamerlan the Mighty. Everyone from here to Voroshilovsky Raion knows Tamerlan. Where's your respect, you fucking goat?"

"Are these bottles yours?"

"Fuck you, goat."

"If they aren't yours, you won't mind if I do this, then." The man grabbed a bottle from under the Mighty's feet and poured its contents into the nearest trash bin.

"You motherfucker!"

Before the Mighty could exact his revenge, a police officer appeared. The same officer, Paul realized, who had stolen his money earlier in the night.

"What is this?" the cop asked.

"We are the Lion Brigade," answered the leader of the brigade.

"And what the hell is that?" asked the cop.

"We are a patriotic youth social movement opposed to drinking alcoholic beverages in public spaces. These men are in violation of the law of the Russian Federation. We have it all on camera: Drinking and smoking in public spaces and non-designated smoking zones. When I emptied their alcohol for them, I was threatened with violence. Oh, and you're on YouTube."

Upon learning this, the officer turned to the closest camera and smiled.

One of the Lion Brigade members pulled out a plastic spray bottle and shot a stream of water on the lit cigarette of one of the brothers.

"I'm sick of you black asses as it is," the cop said to the Caucasians. He called for backup and two other officers appeared. At once, the three pulled out their nightsticks and went about crushing Caucasian flesh and bone.

The Mighty cursed his way down to the pavement.

In between lashings, the cop looked up, locking eyes with Paul. "You!"

"Oh, fuck."

Paul ran, knocking down cameraman two during his escape. He kept on through the park, down the path and around individuals and couples, until he met with a Russian youth crouched over, tying his shoe.

Paul tripped, this time doing a full summersault before landing on his side.

His head was pounding. His knee was in agony. He popped another painkiller into his mouth. Then another.

Walking home was out of the question. He would call a taxi. He tapped his address into the app and waited. A longer than normal search brought nothing.

"Fucking Yandex," he mumbled.

His phone vibrated in his hand. The vibration had been so violent he nearly threw his phone across the street. Another text from Olga. This one a pouty-faced selfie. *Where are youuuuu?*

As it was now, White Horse was only slightly closer than his apartment. And the toilet situation there was very likely the same—or worse—than at Black Dog. He popped a painkiller into his mouth, then another, and limped off toward the bridge. Cops were out in high numbers tonight, and Paul hoped, so long as he kept his head down, he could escape notice.

A clatter nearby brought him to a stop a hundred or so feet from the bridge. He scanned the area, his gaze eventually falling on an elderly woman, gaunt and haggard, skirt hiked up around her waist, perched atop a trashcan outside an open produkty. After shitting her brains out in full view of the public along one of Volgograd's busiest streets, she hopped down to the sidewalk and shook her head in the same classic gesture that she and so many her mentally deranged kin had perfected while begging for money.

Paul could cry, imagining that, once upon a time, before the madness had set in, these women might have lived a more or less normal life. The woman he just saw had once been somebody's daughter, after all. Perhaps somebody's sister or mother. For all he knew—or she knew, for that matter—she could be some kid's long, very lost babushka.

With a sigh, Paul continued forward and onto the bridge, immediately catching sight of two individuals moving toward him.

The Mormons? At this hour? *Kill me now.*

As the two drew near, Paul heaved a sigh of relief. The young men were obviously drunk—and therefore *not* Mormon—staggering and swaying their way across the bridge.

As they were about to pass, Paul went right to avoid a collision.

"Mate!" one of them called out.

Paul kept walking.

"Mate!" the other called out.

The path was blocked.

"Mate, you crawlin' tonight?" The blond twentysomething, scruffy and wearing flip-flops, delivered the question in a thick Australian accent.

"Am I crawling tonight?"

"Maaate!" said his compatriot—shorter, with broad shoulders and a mess of untamed brown hair. "It's a seppo!"

"A what?" asked Paul.

"You American, mate?"

"Yeah."

"Well cheers, ya bogan." He pointed a thumb to his blond buddy. "Me and my mate Kenny here are just a couple of bogans trying to crawl."

"We've been crawlin' since Budapest mate," Kenny said. "Actually, I've been crawlin' since Prague back in '09."

"Mate, I heard Prague '09 made Budapest '12 look like Perth '11."

"Reckon?"

"What's crawling?" Paul asked.

"Maaaate," they said in unison.

"Reckon this bogan's never crawled," said not Kenny. "Pub crawlin', mate. You crawlin' tonight?"

"I'm just trying to get home."

"Piss on that," Kenny said. "Me and Bruce here are just waiting on our mate Deacon, then we're going to crawl."

"Deacon's a legend mate," Bruce said. "Despite being totally povvo, he's been crawlin' with us for years. I've seen that cunt drink thirty-six beers in Budapest."

"Deacon loves beers, doesn't he?" Kenny said.

"Mate," Bruce returned. "Know what else Deacon loves? Babylons, mate. Sheilas with big soft babylons."

"Come on, mate." Kenny draped an arm over Paul's shoulder and pulled him away from the bridge. "Wait for Deacon to crawl on over. You'll love that cunt."

Suddenly lightheaded, Paul fought the urge to lie down right there on the bridge to stop the world from spinning. It nearly overcame his urge to shit. Nearly.

"The yank looks tired, Bruce."

"Reckon he needs some Vicky Bazzas."

Paul looked from one to the other. "Vicky Bazzas?"

Bruce laughed. "Strayan beer, ya ignorant twit."

The three ended up outside a small produkty, where Kenny stopped a passing Russian. "Ey, mate. Ya crawlin' tonight?"

"What?" the Russian responded in English.

"Crawlin'?"

"What is crawlin'?"

"You know, mate. Grab a few pints in one pub, then a few pints in another. Then you kind of just keep doing it. If there are any sheilas, you can look at their babylons."

"Deacon loves sheilas with nice babylons," Bruce added.

"Who is this . . . Deacon?" the Russian asked.

"Deacon's a legend!" Kenny replied.

"I do not understand you." The Russian walked off.

"What a bogan," Kenny said.

"What a cunt," Bruce said.

Kenny went inside the produkty. From outside, Paul witnessed what appeared to be a heated discussion between Kenny and the guy behind the counter.

A moment later, Kenny emerged, beer-less. "Mate, that dickhead, like, tried to put his authority on me. No selling of booze after eleven? What rubbish is that? Let's see if these cunts have any Vicky Bazzas."

Paul turned his attention across the street to a small army of people, perhaps thirty or forty in all, carrying giant flags representing who they were and what they stood for. Was today a national holiday? Was he not told something about that earlier? Russia celebrated more public holidays than any other four countries combined, and, for the life of him, Paul could never keep track. They didn't matter so much to him as his school required that he teach on most holidays, or, at least, make up for a holiday by working a Saturday. Many of these holidays tended to take a dark turn, bringing out in force Russia's nationalists, who seemed always looking for a reason to exact violence in and among their communities. When he managed to remember them, Paul usually opted to avoid public spaces on these days.

"*Slava Rossii!*"

This was the rallying cry of the nationalists across the street, where several individuals were shouting derogatory edicts about Jews and Caucasians.

"Let's see if these cunts have any Vicky Bazzas," Kenny said.

"No, no," Paul said. "I wouldn't—"

Kenny pushed Paul forward. "Let's go, mate!"

The nationalists wore a range of attire—some in camo, others in tracksuits, some shirtless with their tattoos on display. Cigarette smoke permeated the already hot, thick air.

Kenny staggered up to the group. "How ya bloody going, ya bogans?"

The nationalists turned a collective gaze on the newcomers. The silence was deafening. For about twenty seconds.

A shirtless guy spoke up. "*Chyo*?"

"No drama, no worries, mate. I'm Kenny, and this is my mate Bruce. We're just a couple of backpackers crawlin' our way across Europe, mate."

"Where you from?" another, wearing a proper Adidas tracksuit, asked.

The nationalists began to encircle the loud English speakers.

"Which you from? Now! Tell now!"

"Straya, mate," Kenny said.

"Straya? What is?"

"You having a laugh, mate? Perth—home to the greatest pub crawl in the world. Australia, mate."

Tracksuit nodded. "Ah, Hugh Jackman."

"Yeah, that cunt's one of ours."

A young woman, petite and seeming out of place among the rest, made her way to the front of the group. "This is good. We think maybe you are Americans. In that case, would be very bad."

"Ah, Christ no, Sheila," Bruce said. "We're no seppos."

"What is seppos?" asked Tracksuit.

"Yanks, mate," Bruce replied. "Americans. Septic tank rhymes with yank."

"My name Vsevolod." He gestured to the group. "We are Russian patriots. We don't like Jews, black-ass Chechens, or fucking Americans."

"Good on you, mate," Bruce said. "We don't like Americans either. One time I was crawlin' in Tallinn and there was this American bloke. I asked 'im, 'How many beers ya having?' and he said, 'Just one or two.' I said, 'Come off it, mate. Are you even crawlin' tonight?' He said, 'Just the one.' And I said, 'Mate, when Deacon gets here, we're gonna have sixteen amber beverages each. Deacon's a legend, mate. See the sheilas here? He'll be after each one of 'em. He likes all these Russian sheilas in Estonia. He likes their babylons most.' While waiting for the cunt, some blokes from the hostel we were staying at set up a game of Never Have I Ever. The main cunt, either Damo or Dazza, said, 'Mates, come in close and listen. I know a lot of this game revolves around sex, but hear me out. You know what my favorite part of a Sheila is? Her vagina, mates.' After that, I went to the bar and asked for the mate's rate, but the cunt wouldn't give it to me. Deacon wound up getting on the wrong bus and ended up at the Russian border. You cunts had a laugh giving him a hard time."

"I don't understand at all," Vsevolod said.

"No drama no worries, mate," Bruce said. "One time I was crawlin' in Tallinn and there was this American bloke. I asked 'im, 'How many beers ya having?' and he said, 'Just one or two.' I said, 'Come off it, mate. Are you even crawlin' tonight?' He said, 'Just the one.' And I said, 'Mate, when Deacon gets here, we're gonna have sixteen amber beverages each. Deacon's a legend, mate. See the sheilas here? He'll be after each one of 'em. He likes all these Russian sheilas in Estonia. He likes their babylons most.' While waiting for the cunt, some blokes from the hostel we were staying at set up a game of Never Have I Ever. The main cunt, either Damo or Dazza, said, 'Mates, come in close and listen. I know a lot of this game revolves around sex, but hear me out. You know what my favorite part of a Sheila is? Her vagina, mates.' After that, I went to the bar and asked for the mate's rate, but the cunt wouldn't give it to me. Deacon wound up getting on the wrong bus and ended up at the Russian border. You cunts had a laugh giving him a hard time."

"What?" asked Vsevolod.

"Are you some kind of fuckwit, mate?" Kenny asked. "What happened was Bruce was crawlin' in Tallinn and there was this American bloke. Wait a second Bruce, you bogan, you forgot about the Latvian cunt. Let's start over. For context. What happened was —"

"I am nationalist. I also football hooligan. Do you like football in Australia?"

"Yeah, mate!" Kenny said. "Melbourne United."

"Yes, I think I know this club. Can ask question?"

"Mate," Kenny said.

"In Russia, we have problem. Too many fucking immigrants. I want to crush them at the sight of them. Russia is for Russians! You have such problem in Australia?"

"Mate, we've got abbo problems and lebbo problems."

"Lebbo, what is lebbo?"

"Mate, reckon me and Bruce are trying to grab a feed in Perth. We don't want Maccas or Keffas, we want a lebbo pizza. They tell us it's not called lebbo pizza. I say, 'Mate, you don't even crawl. Just give us a lebbo pizza.' Then the cunt says, 'No alcohol here.' This, after we order some Vicky Bazzas. I say, 'At least give us the mate's rate.' He says, 'No mate's rate.' It's like, if you don't crawl, then crawl back to Lebostan, you brown cunt."

"Yes, I understand you." Vsevolod pulled out his phone. "I show you something,"

"Maybe wait till Deacon gets here?" Bruce said.

Kenny gave him a shove. "Just look at what he wants to bloody show us, mate."

Vsevolod turned the screen to them and swiped through several photos.

Paul peered over Kenny's shoulder at the photos of two young men, their faces bloodied to a pulp—worse than his own. The faces, he realized with a queasy feeling, were those of John and Michael, the rival English teachers. The fuckboys. They were going to be hurting for a while—perhaps longer than Paul.

"These Americans walk by us, and we beat them up. This one," he said, pointing to John, "say, 'Sorry, sorry.' I ask, 'Why sorry?' He shrug shoulders. I beat him harder. I beat other one. He say, 'But I'm a cicerone. I have cicerone training.' It did not save him. I am nationalist. I am patriot. I don't like foreigns and other race. Tell me, if I go to the Australia, will they see me as white?"

Kenny shook his head. "I'm sorry, mate. No. There, you're the same as a bloody lebbo or Greek. Definitely not white."

"I am very sad."

"Don't be, mate. You beat up some yanks. Good on you, ya cunt,"

"Yes," Vsevolod said. "That was good feeling. During beating, I say, 'Why do Americans think they won Second World War?' American say, 'Well, technically—,' and I punch him in throat."

"I'll tell you who won World War Two," Kenny said. "Straya."

Bruce gave an endorsing nod. "Reckon everyone knows that."

The nationalist's eyes turned about, doing a mental exercise. "Guys, I am too tired now. Maybe I go to home to bed."

"Piss on that, ya wog." Bruce spit on the ground. "Deacon's not even here yet. Hasn't told you about his dad's Google history. You're bloody crawlin' tonight."

"Okay, I wait for Deacon." Vsevolod's eyes cleared and zeroed in on Paul. "You. Why you so quiet?"

All around them, the patriotic celebration had raged on,

no signs of withering, with more joining in the festivities.

Until that point, Paul had believed himself invisible. "I'm not feeling very well," he said.

"Then you must to drink."

Paul pushed Vsevolod's open bottle of vodka away from his face. "No, thank you."

"You say no? On patriotic holiday? What is problem?"

"Problem is he's a fucking yank," Bruce said.

"Yank?"

Kenny stared up at Vsevolod, a slow smile spreading across his face. "Show him what happens to seppo cunts, ya cunt."

Paul pointed to no one in particular. "Is that a Jew?"

When Vsevolod turned, Paul snatched the bottle of half-empty vodka and smashed it over the nationalist's head.

Then he ran. Knees burning, legs buckling, head throbbing, shit brewing—he ran.

When finally he came to stop, Paul found himself in an alley stuffed with trash, cardboard boxes, discarded microwaves, stray cats, and possibly even skeletons. He didn't recognize the area. It was as if he had crossed over some imaginary border, leaving Volgograd behind, and had run straight into another dimension.

Other than cats doing cat things, the streets were quiet.

A glance around gave him the sense that, at this point, this place was as good as any to take a dump. No matter that there was nothing to wipe with—though, momentarily, he had considered using one of the cats.

He found the darkest corner, backed in, and dropped his

pants. He got a text from Olga. He couldn't bring himself to look. Just like the city had defeated the Germans in 1943, he too had lost the fight.

A few feet ahead, two cats, yowling with fright, shot out from behind a pile of junk. A long shadow followed, the outline of a man, Paul realized, his face obscured by the dark. He pulled two vials from his coat pocket—glowing, pulsating, one red, one green—and emptied them into a large crack in the pavement.

He straightened, and turned toward Paul. "What are you doing?"

Pantless and nearly paralyzed, Paul let loose a nervous chuckle. "It's what it looks like."

"Come with me."

The stranger stepped close enough for Paul to make out a pleasant, moon-shaped face.

"You'll let me use your toilet?"

"Please, come."

"Dear God, thank you."

Paul followed the man, pudgy and looking to be in his mid-thirties, inside a nearby apartment building and to a dimly lit stairwell. Up and up they climbed, until, finally, at the fifth floor, the man ventured down a darkened hallway and stopped in front of a door about halfway down.

As the man struggled with the deadbolt, he noticed Paul's trembling leg. "Please," he said. "Be patient."

By the time they entered the apartment, Paul's bowels were sounding the alarm bell—so close, he was, finally, to relief.

"Please, take off shoes."

Paul, clenching his jaw, as well as another part of his

anatomy, did as he was told.

"I am Vassily," the man said.

"Paul. I don't mean to be rude, Vassily, but I really must use your toilet."

"Yes, yes. I see that. You are so lucky I find you."

"Very lucky," Paul said. "And eternally grateful. Which way is the toilet?"

Paul glanced toward the kitchen. There were vials everywhere—some empty, but most filled with bright, radiating liquid. In addition, there was a mass of tangled wiring, as well as a collection of machine parts, covering nearly every inch of counter space.

"Let me ask a question from my heart. Do you have girlfriend, Paul? Wife?"

"What?" Paul shifted his weight. "I really, really need to use your bathroom. It's coming. It's coming!"

"Yes, yes. It's coming," Vassily said with a nod. "Do you have a woman?"

"No!"

"But you do like women?"

"I like toilets!" Paul cried.

"What is the biggest problem facing women today?"

"I don't know!" Paul said, his face growing hot. "Not being allowed to use the toilet?"

"No. The biggest problem facing women today is a problem that becomes an issue for men as well."

Vassily drew his phone from his back pocket and turned the screen toward Paul.

Asses. Photo after photo of female asses. Some in

thongs, some in yoga pants, others in nothing at all. Asses, asses, everywhere.

"What do you think?" Vassily said.

"I think asses are the last thing I want to be thinking about right now." *Except where I'd like to put my own!*

"Exactly." Vassily said. "You are repulsed. And why? Because you have to shit." He moved into the kitchen. "In last decade, thanks to Instagram and Snapchat, ass has become more popular than tits. The popularity of ass-eating has also skyrocketed. I cannot explain this phenomenon. I only observe. And invent. Everyone loves ass. But you—you are repulsed when I show you photos because you have to shit and all your mind can think right now is how badly you need to shit. Never mind these asses, you say. But, perhaps, you're thinking about these beautiful female asses shitting. No man wants to think about that, ever. In this world we spend ninety-nine percent of our time under illusion that beautiful women with beautiful women asses do not shit. You can believe me. I am a man of science." He held up a vial containing a dark, sludgy, shit-green substance. "My benefactor, whose name is definitely *not* Rocco Siffreddi, is paying me lot of money for this."

"What the—"

"This is the cure," Vassily said. "This will stop women from needing to shit. Ever."

Fuck me. "Please, Vassily. Just let me use your toilet."

"It is fateful I came across you. While this substance will be marketed to females, I still have yet to test it on a live subject. I cannot think of better subject than you, Paul. I cannot let you use my toilet. But I also don't want you shitting on my floor."

"You fucking lunatic! Just let me use your bathroom!"

Vassily held out the vial to Paul, who by now was drenched with sweat and shaking all over. Even if he tried to run to the toilet now, he would never make it.

This entire shitstorm of a night, he now realized, had led him to this "fateful" moment.

He swiped the vial from Vassily's hand. "What's in it?"

"Does it matter?"

With a sneer, Paul tilted back his head and threw the contents down his throat.

His throat, in reply, dried up and began to close. Seconds later, it was as if the whole of his insides were closing in on themselves. Paul felt a jolt low in his abdomen, as if his colon was clearing itself by shitting its contents back up into his stomach.

"Step toward me," Vassily said.

Paul did as told, noticing the absence of a certain discomfiting sensation.

"How do you feel?"

"Weird. Off."

"But do you have to shit?"

Paul hesitated, then shook his head.

~~~

"And he never shit again."

The coffee on my shirt was dry. Only slightly sticky now. I looked up at the students. One of the six, I noted, had fled.

"What do you mean he never shit again?" Chris asked.

"And whatever happened with Olga or the guy who punched his ear in half?" Forrest asked.
~~~

"What the hell is a lebbo?"

"Lebostan?"

"I don't know," I said with a shrug. "The story just kind of ends."

Russia Cop

Five Documentaries You Need to See at the Venice Film Festival

By Gale Finkelstein

If previous years are any indication, Venice is making a habit of showcasing strong documentaries. Gianfranco Rosi's Italian documentary *Sacro GRA* set the stage when it became the first documentary feature to take the top prize back in 2013. This year, the competition is fierce, with two documentaries from two equally young filmmakers in the running.

The first, from American filmmaker and enfant terrible Rudy Pingas (who also stars), is titled *From Cisgender Novice to Master Cicerone* and details the filmmaker's journey as a straight male through the hardships and pitfalls of master Cicerone training. One participant who appeared in the film told journalists: "Its passage rate is less than forty percent. Even the California and New York State Bar Exams have higher success rates. There were Navy Seals with us who found the training too difficult. I'm lucky to be alive." Early buzz indicates a film that is harrowing, suspenseful, and stranger than fiction and makes the boot camp sequence from *Full Metal Jacket* look like *Paddington.*

The second documentary feature, with the uninspired title of *Russia Cop*, has the misfortune of being the second documentary about Russia Cop out this year. Reminiscent of 1998's *Deep Impact* versus *Armageddon* box office battle, Ukrainian filmmaker Anna Pavlyuchenko's feature comes just three months after Werner Herzog's *From Russia Cop with Love* captivated audiences. Herzog brought his trademark Verité to the story of Russia Cop, showing a side to Russia and Russian politics rarely available to Western audiences. Furthermore, Herzog's film showed a side of Russia Cop not shown in the media, a more human and, daresay, gentle side. Pavlyuchenko's film, on the other hand, has already generated buzz of being nothing more than anti-Russian propaganda from a Ukrainian nationalist. And if the trailers are to be believed, the film is a simple rehashing of clips from the media, amounting to little more than showing what's already readily available on the internet.

Pavlyuchenko first impressed audiences with her first feature documentary, *Chernobyl Babies*, when she was only nineteen years old. Her career seemed extremely promising until two films later, the trend of going out of her way to demonize Russia at every opportunity became apparent. Then rumors began to circulate that she had connections with various Ukrainian nationalist groups. While the filmmaker certainly possesses talent, it's hard to be excited about her upcoming feature when Herzog's film has already established itself as the definitive film on the story of Russia Cop.

This year's sole Australian entry, *The Rape of Darren Merriman,* chronicles the life of paint-sniffing survivor Darren . . .

Part One

EXT. PALACE SQUARE - DAY

Crowds of people walk to and fro or stand in groups with the backdrop of the Hermitage behind them.

ANNA (V.O.)

The Russian Soul. What is it? Can it be understood? For generations foreigners and Russians alike have asked this question. But what exactly is it? Is there one accepted interpretation?

CUT TO:

EXT. PALACE SQUARE - DAY

A middle-aged man is being interviewed with an off-camera hand holding a mic up to his face.

ANNA (O.C.)

What does the phrase "Russian Soul" mean to you?

MIDDLE-AGED INTERVIEWEE

It's the Tyutchev quote, isn't it? "Russia cannot be understood with the mind alone, No ordinary yardstick can span her greatness: She stands alone, unique -In Russia, one can only believe."

It's our ideals. The moral and heroic behavior of our people throughout history.

ANNA (O.C.)

Can a foreigner ever grasp these ideals or understand this the way a Russian can?

MIDDLE-AGED INTERVIEWEE

Of course the answer is no. It's a phenomenon unique to Russia and its people.

CUT TO:

EXT. PALACE SQUARE - DAY

A middle-aged woman is being interviewed with an off-camera hand, holding a mic up to her face.

MIDDLE-AGED INTERVIEWEE FEMALE

Russian Soul is what makes our literature and art and performances the best in the world. You know, I've been to England many times. They have theater and ballet, but it isn't the same. Their performances lack what makes a performance transcendent, as opposed to merely good. Only in Russia can you find ballet that is truly transcendent and can be truly labeled as art.

CUT TO:

EXT. PALACE SQUARE - DAY

A man in his early twenties is being interviewed.

YOUNG MAN

It's about friendship, I think. I had a friend who studied abroad in Prague and another in the UK. They said the people there don't really know what friendship means. People get strange if you call them on the phone without warning them.

They think it's weird if you want to talk to them every day or invite them to your place for family meals. With Russians, we have deep affections in our friendships. We don't call someone a friend if that is only a person we see once a week and have small talk with. Friendship between Russians means laying your soul bare to one another.

CUT TO:

EXT. NEVSKY PROSPEKT - DAY

People walk the busy Saint Petersburg Boulevard. Canals can be seen in the distance.

ANNA (V.O.)

We received many such answers as to the nature of the Russian Soul. Whether it was about bonds and friendship, heroic deeds, a blind belief in sheer luck, an ability to survive in severe conditions, nostalgia, or simply being incomprehensible to outsiders, all of the answers provided showed that the people of Russia believe in their uniqueness among the peoples of the world. From an outside perspective, Winston Churchill described Russia as "a riddle wrapped in a mystery inside an enigma." But why are we talking about Russian Soul? In order to understand the enigmatic inventor, Vassily Gladyshev, one first must pose that question. For the record, I am not from Russia. Rather, I was born and grew up in Kyiv. For the past two years, the focus of my documentaries has been on Russia. My name is Anna Pavlyuchenko, and in this video, we have been granted access given to very few--a sit-down with Vassily Gladyshev.

FADE TO BLACK.

FADE IN:

EXT. VOLGOGRAD - DAY

An aerial view shows the city of Volgograd. The Rodina-Mat monument is visible.

ANNA (V.O.)

Today we are meeting with inventor Vassily Gladyshev in his home, in the city of Volgograd.

CUT TO:

EXT. VOLGOGRAD STREET - DAY

The camera follows Anna from behind as she traverses streets with apartments on either side. She avoids various puddles and potholes.

ANNA (V.O.) (CONT'D)

Famously, he does not grant interviews, but he has agreed to meet with us. Before speaking with the man himself, we wanted to get as full a picture of the person as we could. To do this, we spoke to those who know him or who have purchased his products.

Anna approaches Gladyshev's place. It is small and unremarkable.

CUT TO:

INT. OFFICE - DAY

A close-up on Vadim's face. He is in his late thirties/early forties. The camera pulls back to reveal him sitting in an office.

ANNA (O.C.)

Why are we talking to you today?

VADIM

Because I am a victim of one of Vassily Gladyshev's products.

ANNA (O.C.)

Victim?

VADIM

Precisely.

ANNA (O.C.)

Tell us what happened.

VADIM

I wasn't aware of the Popcorn Belt fiasco. Had I been, I would have known of the toxicity associated with Vassily Gladyshev's name.

ANNA (O.C.)

Which product did you purchase?

VADIM

Is that a joke?

The camera pulls back to reveal a cartoonishly large bulge in Vadim's pants.

CUT TO:

INT. OFFICE NUMBER TWO - DAY

In a similar-looking office sits Vladimir. He is in his late twenties.

ANNA (O.C.)

Can you tell us who you are?

VLADIMIR

I'm Vladimir. I'm twenty-six years old. Engineer. I live in Saint Petersburg.

ANNA (O.C.)

Are you married?

VLADIMIR

No, I'm not married.

ANNA (O.C.)

Why are we talking to you today?

VLADIMIR

I bought a Vassily Gladyshev product.

ANNA (O.C.)

Which one?

There is a pause.

VLADIMIR

The Penis Enlarger 9000.

ANNA (O.C.)

Had you ever bought a similar product?

VLADIMIR

Never.

ANNA (O.C.)

So why this one?

VLADIMIR

Look, as a man of science, I'm very skeptical by nature. All these enhancement pills are nonsense. I researched the science on this one. It seemed . . . sound, and, well, I was desperate.

ANNA (O.C.)

Did it work?

VLADIMIR

Yes, very much so.

ANNA (O.C.)

What's the problem, then? Why are you suing Vassily Gladyshev?

The camera pulls back to reveal Vladimir holding hands with a man.

CUT TO:

INT. VALENTIN'S APARTMENT - DAY

An elderly married couple sits at their kitchen table. This is Galina Petrovna and Valentin Illyich. They are Vladimir's parents.

GALINA PETROVNA

When our Vovechka came home to us with Ruslan, we knew something terrible had happened. He had always been a shy boy, but a homosexual? Impossible! Then, on the news, everywhere you looked, people were filing lawsuits against Vassily Gladyshev. Sons and husbands were being turned into gays left and right. Gay, impotent, or having unpatriotic thoughts.

ANNA (O.C.)

Vladimir told us he's uncontrollably in love with Ruslan.

VALENTIN ILLYICH

Both Vova and Ruslan are good boys. Ruslan has been very helpful around the house. He helped us fix our sink the other day. Galya was in the middle of fixing him dinner when I forgot that he is a fucking faggot. I demand that my son get fixed.

ANNA (O.C.)

Fixed by Gladyshev?

VALENTIN ILLYICH

I'm afraid he'd just make things worse.

The camera lingers on the old married couple.

CUT TO BLACK.

FADE IN:

EXT. VOLGOGRAD - MORNING

The sun rises over the city of Volgograd.

ANNA (V.O.)

Just who is Vassily Gladyshev, you may ask? Just two years ago, he was completely anonymous. Now, he's the most famous man in Russia.

CUT TO:

INT. NEWSROOM - EVENING

A male news anchor, forties, sits next to his female co-anchor and reads the report.

NEWSANCHOR

Meet the self-proclaimed Russian Elon Musk.

CUT TO:

EXT. CITY STREET - NIGHT

Vassily Gladyshev, late thirties, exits a building and is immediately surrounded by journalists and photographers. He seems uneasy.

CUT TO:

EXT. APARTMENT COURTYARD - DAY

Anton, late thirties, sits on a bench in the courtyard. Pigeons are feeding on the ground around him.

ANTON

He was always calling himself the next Elon Musk, or the Russian Elon Musk.

ANNA (O.C.)

Clarify who you are please.

ANTON

My name is Anton. I went to school with Vassily since the first grade.

ANNA (O.C.)

What was he like?

ANTON

He was always making things.

ANNA (O.C.)

What kinds of things?

ANTON

Honestly, pretty useless things. When we were younger, we thought it was kind of cool, you know? Just the fact that he was building things. But as we got older, we realized everything he built was pretty stupid and useless.

CUT TO:

EXT. VOLGOGRAD STREET - DAY

Anna approaches Vassily's apartment building. She stops and examines the building.

ANNA

Can this really be it? It doesn't look right.

CAMERAMAN (O.C.)

I'm not so sure.

An unassuming man, late thirties, walks by with a small dog at the end of a leash.

ANNA

Excuse me, this might be a strange question, but does Vassily Gladyshev live in one of these buildings?

CUT TO:

INT. VASSILY'S APARTMENT - DAY

Vassily sits at his kitchen table. His dog is scratching at his legs.

ANNA (O.C.)

How long have you lived here?

VASSILY

Only a couple of months. I know what you're thinking. It's a dump. I agree, but it's got a bed, a fridge. There's a park where I can walk Belka.

ANNA (O.C.)

Rumor is you had a house in—

VASSILY (INTERUPTING ANNA)

Yes.

ANNA (O.C.)

We've heard accounts from people who knew you and people who used your products, but we'd like to hear your tale from your own mouth. Please, tell us as much as you can.

There is a pause.

VASSILY

I've always liked making things. Since I was little, I always had trouble sleeping.

CUT TO:

INT. HOUSE - EVENING

Home video footage of Vassily as a little kid putting Legos together. Vassily's voice plays over the footage.

VASSILY (V.O.)

My mind never stopped coming up with ideas. It didn't know how to rest.

CUT TO:

INT. VASSILY'S APARTMENT - DAY

Belka the dog now rests in Vassily's lap.

ANNA (O.C.)

You speak about your mind and you as if you are two separate things.

VASSILY

It feels that way.

ANNA (O.C.)

Your first invention was the Penis Enlarger 8000?

VASSILY

Nine thousand. And no, that wasn't the first.

ANNA (O.C.)

What was?

VASSILY

(Sighs)

The Popcorn Belt. I was only seventeen when I made it.

ANNA (O.C.)

I'd heard rumors, but that was actually you?

CUT TO:

INT. MOVIE THEATER AUDITORIUM

A cheap-looking commercial is playing. A crowd is exiting the screening of a movie. A sad and pathetic-looking teenager looks at all the popcorn on the ground and in the seats.

CUT TO:

INT. MOVIE THEATER AUDITORIUM

The commercial continues. The movie ends and the lights come on. Audience members are seen with popcorn all over their shirts and pants. They sigh and look deeply disappointed. Several shake their heads in disapproval.

COMMERCIAL NARRATOR (V.O.)

(In English)

Are you tired of this happening to you? Are you tired of all that delicious popcorn going to waste? Are you sick of having to wash your pants every time you come home from seeing a movie? Say goodbye to your problems because we have just the thing for you film buffs!

CUT TO:

INT. MOVIE THEATER AUDITORIUM

The movie watchers here are happy and smiling. They greedily shove popcorn into their mouths without worry as they can all be seen wearing the Popcorn Belt. The belt goes around their waists with a net extending about eight inches outward. The popcorn that misses their mouths falls onto the net. One viewer drops their popcorn, laughs when they see it landing safely in their net, and picks it up to eat it.

CUT TO:

INT. MOVIE THEATER AUDITORIUM

Various shots of clean auditorium floors and chairs. The custodian smiles and whistles while he examines the sparkling clean space. He shrugs and smiles at the camera.

COMMERCIAL NARRATOR (V.O.)
(CONT'D)

Never waste your buttery, delicious treat again!

CUT TO BLACK.

CUT TO:

INT. VASSILY'S APARTMENT - DAY

Vassily sits in silence with his head down.

VASSILY

This would never work in Russia. The idea from the very beginning was to release it in the US. When it came out, there was mild enthusiasm. We just couldn't compel people to care. With such a weak level of interest, we started hiring plants, wearing the product, to be present in theaters. Then, suddenly, more than we could have ever predicted, the demand for the Popcorn Belt skyrocketed. I was happy, the company was happy, the moviegoers were happy. Then . . .

ANNA (O.C.)

And then what happened?

VASSILY

It was the prevalence of (censored). McAllen-Edinburg-Mission, Texas. That is America's fattest city. On that August day, over fifty percent of the viewers there were wearing a Popcorn Belt. Eighty percent of the viewers were morbidly obese. Five minutes into the movie, there was an electrical fire. None of the viewers were able to get out of their rows. Every overweight viewer wearing a Popcorn Belt got stuck in their seat. Two hundred people burned to death. Russia refused to introduce the product domestically, and I was out of a job.

ANNA (O.C.)

Did that failure lead to you creating the Penis Enlarger?

VASSILY

You have to understand. It wasn't a dream of mine to work in the sex or body-modification industry. But I must create. My brain must create. I'm addicted to creating. Therefore, I look at what hasn't been done yet and what needs to be done. Do you know how many performance- and size-enhancing pills exist for men? I wanted to create something real. No trickery or false claims. I spent the next two years developing a tablet, no surgery necessary, just a tablet that would arouse natural growth in the penis. We even set the limit so that, whoever you were, the natural growth limit would be five-and-a-half centimeters. Think about it.

If you're already eighteen centimeters, twenty-three-and-a-half is a bit on the ridiculous side. If you're twelve-and-a-half centimeters, five-and-a-half makes you eighteen and you're a satisfied customer. If you're seven-and-a-half, that's essentially a micro-penis. Thirteen centimeters isn't huge, but it's certainly an ego booster and markedly better than seven-and-a-half.

CUT TO:

INT. OFFICE - DAY

Vadim is sitting and looking worn out.

VADIM

I hadn't had sex in years. All I wanted was . . . to be a little bigger. This is what I got.

The camera pans to the large bulge in his pants.

VADIM

It won't fit inside anything. I can't even pleasure myself. Each time, too much blood rushes down, and I pass out. No surgeon in the world will operate.

CUT TO:

INT. VALENTIN'S APARTMENT - DAY

GALINA PETROVNA

He turned our baby boy into a gay.

VALENTIN ILLYICH

When I see my boy fixing the sink or bringing in groceries or watching television, I see nothing unusual. But then I realize he's doing all of those things while gay.

CUT TO:

INT. VASSILY'S APARTMENT - DAY

VASSILY

I was desperate. It wasn't for the money. It was never about the money. It was the need to create. It's like a drug. Around that time, sex dolls were getting really lifelike, and I thought, why not make one that's actually alive? Your very own living, breathing sex doll with a heartbeat? No matter how lifelike a doll may look, there will always be that uncanny valley effect. They have those shark eyes. I also considered the fact that with these living, breathing sex dolls, it would put naturally born women who turn to prostitution at less risk. I fear for the women who end up in the sex trade. So what did I do? I conducted a survey. I looked at the most popular porn videos, most prolific porn actresses, most searched videos and tags, looked at Instagram models with the most followers, etc. With this information, I was going to create the world's most fuckable woman. This isn't to say she would necessarily be the most beautiful woman, but according to search results, the woman that men most wanted to have sex with. A real, living woman. But obviously, I didn't want to wait eighteen years for this human to develop and grow. My team and I created memories, and as far as the brain was concerned, it was a real, conscious human brain, created from stem cells. Real organs, real skin, real hair. Artificial memories and preprogrammed intuitions and drives.

ANNA (O.C.)

Did she have free will?

Vassily is silent.

VASSILY

Yes.

ANNA (O.C.)

This living, breathing woman, designed to be a sex doll with a heartbeat and a consciousness, and can be purchased, had free will?

VASSILY

There is an epidemic of loneliness in the world right now. Particularly in the United States, but also in places like Japan and parts of Western Europe. Men are desperate for female attention. Prostitution is illegal in most places, and even in places where it is legal, it's a dangerous game. There's disease and slavery. This project was started with the best of intentions, for men and women alike. This was to give lonely men an opportunity to feel sexually fulfilled, and emotionally as well, without the pressures of society weighing on them.

ANNA (O.C.)

But someone with free will can choose not to have sex if they don't want to. What prevented her from not having sex with her owners?

CUT TO:

INT. LAWYER'S OFFICE - DAY

A handsome, middle-aged lawyer adjusts his tie.

LAWYER

While being human, she wasn't birthed. Nor did she have parents or grow up in the traditional sense. And, because she had a chip implanted in her brain that told her her function in life was to fulfill the sexual desires of her owner, traditional human rights laws didn't apply to her. She was a patented product created with specific customer satisfaction goals in mind. By law, she was living property, similar to a pet. Think of her as a dog or a cat.

ANNA (O.C.)

A dog or cat that you can fuck?

The lawyer doesn't answer.

CUT TO:

INT. AUDITORIUM - NIGHT

Vassily is onstage in front of a semi-large audience, comprised mostly of Japanese men.

VASSILY

This is the future of sex.

The audience gives a mild round of applause.

CUT TO:

VASSILY'S APARTMENT - DAY

ANNA (O.C.)

You built a woman. The ideal woman to have sex with. But there were no options for add-ons or adjustments?

VASSILY

That would have gone against everything we worked so hard to achieve. If someone had the power to constantly change the size of their breasts, ass, or lips, then the sensation of making love to the world's most sexually appealing woman would go away entirely. Sure, maybe John in Ohio decides her breasts aren't quite as big as he had hoped, but does it stop there? He changes her breasts, then her elbows; eventually it's not the same woman anymore. We had constructed the ideal woman. And we decided to make her nineteen rather than eighteen. Believe it or not, eighteen is still too young for most men, but nineteen is the optimal age of female attractiveness. So Mila had grown to the age of nineteen. No enhancements or upgrades. And for ninety-nine point nine percent of customers, she truly would have been the most beautiful woman they had ever slept with.

ANNA (O.C.)

But that's not how it turned out, is it?

CUT TO:

INT. AUDITORIUM - NIGHT

VASSILY

Gentlemen, I give you . . . MILA.

A young and attractive woman with long legs and large breasts walks out onto the stage. She is wearing a skimpy outfit. She stands next to Vassily, and the audience erupts with applause.

VASSILY

Who would like to ask Mila some questions?

Hundreds of excited hands raise up.

CUT TO:

Quick flashes of various news clips and newspaper headlines showing the failure of Vassily's

"Mila."

CUT TO:

INT. JAPANESE OFFICE - EVENING

A Japanese businessman, mid-fifties, slowly inhales a cigarette.

JAPANESE BUSINESSMAN

She just stands there saying no. Every time I try to touch her, she slaps my hand away. I call customer support, to no avail. I'm no rapist, but eventually I try getting aggressive. In that case, she curls up into a ball, and it's impossible to unlock her limbs. I paid twelve thousand dollars for this!

CUT TO:

INT. VASSILY'S APARTMENT - DAY

ANNA (O.C.)

What happened with Mila?

VASSILY

No matter how much reprogramming we did, the Mila simply wouldn't sleep with the majority of her owners. She refused them and often mocked them to their faces. We don't know where she picked this up, but several customers called, in tears, because she belittled them so cruelly. As it turned out, the explanation the world over from her own mouths was that she only wanted to sleep with very, very attractive men. Ones who were a nine point five or higher on her own scale. That, or incredibly rich. But, in that case, simple successful businessmen wouldn't cut it. She would only sleep with the absolute top one percent. So, the average client, a man who has had bad luck with women and has been lonely a long, long time, spent money beyond their means for Mila. After all that, she wouldn't even sleep with them! Understandably, most of the Milas were returned.

ANNA (O.C.)

What became of them?

VASSILY

They are sentient people. They've been integrated into society.

CUT TO:

Various shots show Milas working in different establishments. Some are working as baristas and waitresses. Others are seen stocking store shelves. One is seen driving a bus.

VASSILY (V.O.)

Many of them integrated into society by working ordinary jobs, but more than fifty percent make their money from OnlyFans.

There are various shots of Milas on the streets, or in bars and cafés, being hit on by ordinary-looking guys. They turn them down each time. One Mila notices an attractive man, Roman, and smiles at him.

CUT TO:

INT. ROMAN'S PLACE - NIGHT

ROMAN

I've dated three Milas. When one starts giving me too much attitude, I break it off with her and find another one.

CUT TO:

Various shots of Russians in cafés and walking along boulevards and in parks. Often there are insert shots of Milas working or interacting with people. All run with Anna's voice-over.

ANNA (O.C.)

Vassily's track record includes several hundred dead Americans, men who claim they were turned gay by using his products, and men whose penises became so large they could no longer use them. After all that, his drive to invent did not diminish.

CUT TO:

EXT. PARK - LATE AFTERNOON

Anna and Vassily walk side by side. Belka is on a leash and stops often to sniff different trees and attempt to interact with other dogs.

VASSILY

Mila was built with a five-year lifespan in mind. In the labs, we discovered that's how long her body could remain nineteen years old. If the customer felt inclined, they could purchase an injection which would give her another two years. It looks like most or all of the Milas will be dead by next year.

ANNA

Are you ready to talk about Russia Cop?

Vassily pauses his steps. His back is to the camera. He turns to face Anna.

VASSILY

Do you know what was missing from all of my previous inventions?

Anna shakes her head.

VASSILY

Patriotism. More concretely, Russian patriotism. Russian Soul. All of my inventions had catered either to foreigners or to perverse interests introduced into this country by foreigners. Russian Soul was the missing ingredient.

He pauses.

CUT TO:

EXT. MOSCOW STREET - DAY

Three twentysomething men approach a car whose driver is attempting to drive down a pedestrian sidewalk. The driver honks the horn aggressively when the youths won't let him pass. The driver rolls down his window.

DENNIS

Why are you driving on the sidewalk?

DRIVER

And who the hell are you?

DENNIS

I'm the head of the movement "Stop a Dickhead."

DRIVER

And what the hell is that?

CUT TO:

INT. DENNIS' APARTMENT - DAY

Dennis is severely bruised and broken. He has two black eyes, a bandage on his head, both arms in slings, and looks much older than when we last saw him.

ANNA (O.C.)

Can you tell us about your movement?

DENNIS

(speaking with difficulty)

We started half a decade ago. It started from my own personal experiences with bad drivers and rude people in Moscow. On one occasion, I waited behind a double-parked car for four hours. These drivers who don't care about anyone but themselves force us to commit traffic violations.

ANNA (O.C.)

Is that how you came up with the idea for the stickers?

DENNIS

The problem with these people is they've gotten away with it for so long they believe they are immune to the law. What could we do to change that?

CUT TO:

EXT. MOSCOW STREET - EVENING

There is a car on the sidewalk with a young female driver who is honking her horn at the four vigilante youths blocking her path.

FEMALE DRIVER

Get out of my way, you fucking idiots! I drive wherever the fuck I want!

DENNIS

And that is why you're going to get this sticker!

FEMALE DRIVER

Don't you dare put that fucking thing on my car!

DENNIS

Get the sticker!

One of the young men unfolds a large, circular sticker and places it on the windshield of the woman's car. The sticker reads, "I am a dick-head. I drive/park wherever I want." The woman screams.

CUT TO:

EXT. MOSCOW STREETS - DAY/NIGHT

A montage of Dennis and his team placing the big stickers on car windshields. The drivers scream, argue, and curse. Some of them cry.

CUT TO:

EXT. MOSCOW STREET - DAY

Back to Dennis's confrontation with the first driver.

DENNIS

If you continue down this sidewalk, we'll place this sticker on your window.

DRIVER

You better fucking not. I'll shoot you. I will fucking shoot you.

The driver pulls out a pistol and aims it at Dennis.

DENNIS

You can threaten all you like. You're in violation of the law. You still have time to go back the way you came and merge onto the street the right way.

DRIVER

Listen to me. I'm a man of the church. I'm a priest. Any road I choose to take is the correct road. You best get out of my way and let me by.

DENNIS

We have the blessing of the president of the Russian Federation.

DRIVER

Horseshit.

The two continue arguing with one another, but the sound becomes nearly inaudible. The camera focuses on a large, imposing figure walking from roughly one hundred meters away. The figure, a man, is about one hundred and ninety-eight centimeters, broadly built, has a large, square face, eyes hidden behind dark shades, and is dressed in a futuristic-looking police uniform. He is walking toward the scene at a slow but determined pace.

The camera pans back to the argument. Both men stop shouting as the police officer (Russia Cop) approaches. When Russia Cop arrives, he stands at attention. He then proceeds to scan the area as if he is a Terminator. He does an about-face toward the car.

RUSSIA COP

Step aside, citizens. This is a job for the police.

Dennis's crew move to the sides. Everyone looks

confused. What they see looks more like an android or movie creation than a real police officer.

RUSSIA COP

Kyrlov Dennis Dmitrievich, you have been convicted of the crime of disrespecting society and insulting religious feelings. This Russian Federation law went into effect in 2013. Your guilt has been determined.

(turns to the priest, who is wielding a pistol)

Father Dyatlov, rest assured your assailant will not go unpunished. Find your way home safely. The Russian Federation thanks you and looks to you for guidance.

(turns to Dennis)

Dennis Dmitrievich, prepare to receive punishment.

Russia Cop, with his left hand, grabs Dennis by the collar of his shirt and lifts him up. Russia Cop then proceeds to punch Dennis in the face multiple times before throwing him to the ground. Russia Cop kicks Dennis in the ribs multiple times. Russia Cop breaks both of Dennis's arms before putting the young man in handcuffs. Russia Cop looks directly into the camera.

CUT TO:

A montage shows the same scene filmed from the cell phones of various people who were on the street that day. Some of these clips are presented on the Russian evening news.

CUT TO:

INT. AUDITORIUM - NIGHT

On a stage in front of a large audience, a panel has been set up. Sitting on the panel are several scientists, politicians, and high-ranking police officers. In their midst sits Vassily Gladyshev.

HIGH-RANKING OFFICER

Without further ado, let us introduce the long-awaited Project 36.

There is murmuring throughout the auditorium. From backstage comes Russia Cop in his brand new, futuristic-looking police uniform. Slowly he approaches the front of the stage, similar to his first appearance. He salutes the panel, then does an about-face and salutes the audience.

HIGH-RANKING OFFICER

Vassily Kuzmich, if you would?

Vassily stands.

VASSILY

This is Project 36. Also known as Law Enforcement Officer Aleksandrovich. Aleksandrovich, what is your prime directive?

RUSSIA COP

To enforce Russian Soul and patriotic sentiment throughout the nation. I enforce the laws of the Russian Federation.

No crime can or will escape my vision. I can see up to six crimes happening at the same time, and by my advanced methods of deduction, I rate them according to severity and tackle the worst one first.

VASSILY

What makes you so different from other beat police officers?

RUSSIA COP

I have only one mission--to stop crime. I have no other desires or needs. I do not sleep. I do not require sustenance. I live only to serve.

VASSILY

That sounds good in theory, but the world is a dangerous place. What happens if you are attacked by multiple assailants or someone stronger than you?

Russia Cop cracks a robotic smile.

From backstage come two enormous muscle freaks of men. Each one is of similar height to Russia Cop but significantly larger in frame. They look like monsters. They stand on either side of Russia Cop and lunge at him. Russia Cop blocks their punches by grasping their fists in his hands. He then lifts them both, simultaneously, off the ground and holds them over his head. He eventually sets them down. At this point, the audience is silent.

VASSILY

If you still aren't convinced . . .

An armed police officer enters the stage. He raises his hand and points his pistol at Russia Cop. Before firing, he glances at the high-ranking officer. The high-ranking officer gives a nod of approval. The officer sets his sights and fires at Russia Cop. The audience gasps. Russia Cop did not defend himself. The camera reveals the impact to Russia Cop's chest, where he was hit. There is a minor dent, but it appears he is uninjured.

RUSSIA COP

You can shoot me all you like. I am immune to bullets.

VASSILY

But how is this possible? Are you a robot? Some kind of android?

RUSSIA COP

I am but flesh and blood. I am human.

VASSILY

How can a human be immune to bullets?

RUSSIA COP

I was conceived by Russian Soul.

There is an audible reaction from the audience. One reporter can no longer bear it and stands up, ready to ask a question.

REPORTER

Vassily Kuzmich, what is this? Please, stop leaving us in the dark.

VASSILY

You see, Aleksandrovich is no machine. He is but a man, like any of us. But unlike any of us, he was conceived by Russian Soul. That very fact makes him stronger, faster, more agile, and yes, immune to bullets.

REPORTER

Are you saying he was created by Russian Soul?

VASSILY

Yes.

REPORTER

But how?

VASSILY

Let's just accept it. My team and I have been hard at work unlocking the code, and we found it. But that isn't what this is about. This is about carrying Russia to a bright and optimistic future. With Aleksandrovich, we no longer need to worry about the nation being led astray. Russian Soul will be at the forefront of our nation's progress. As you will see in the coming weeks, this country is heading toward a very bright future.

The camera stays on Vassily. The noise from the audience is muted. Russia Cop can be seen looming behind him.

ANNA (V.O.)

The era of Russia Cop had begun.

CUT TO:

A montage of foreign-language news media unfolds, from various angles, the previous clip of Russia Cop assaulting Dennis. The camera focuses in on and zooms into the bottom of the screen of one English-language broadcast where the words "Russia Cop" appear along the bottom of the screen.

CUT TO:

EXT. DARK ALLEYWAY - NIGHT

From the POV of a cell phone video, a young man walks into an alley to see four severely beaten men. There is blood on the ground. They all have broken limbs. They are moaning and barely able to move.

PEDESTRIAN WITH CELL PHONE
(O.C.)

Holy shit. No way. What the hell happened here?

A woman can be heard crying. The pedestrian with the cell phone walks over the bodies, careful not to step on them, and finds the young woman, who appears to be in shock.

PEDESTRIAN WITH CELL PHONE
(O.C.)

What the hell happened here? Did you do

this?

The young woman shakes her head.

PEDESTRIAN WITH CELL PHONE

Then what happened?

WOMAN IN SHOCK

I . . . I was being attacked. Then he came . . .

The pedestrian with the cell phone turns and lets out a gasp as he sees Russia Cop emerge from the shadows.

CUT TO:

EXT. CITY CROSSWALK - DAY

Russia Cop can be seen escorting across the street a tiny old woman wearing a shawl. Despite crossing pedestrians, cars come fast, barely avoiding the two. One car zooms by at nearly one hundred and fifteen kilometers per hour. Russia Cop sticks out his hand. The car drives into his outstretched arm. The car flips over Russia Cop and the old woman, landing upside down on the other side of them. Russia Cop completes his mission of escorting the woman across the street. Admirers run up to him.

CUT TO:

EXT. PARK - LATE AFTERNOON

Anna and Vassily are still side by side, walking the dog.

ANNA

Why did he embrace the name Russia Cop? Was it not a typo on British television? Were they not referring to him as "Russian Cop?" And he embraced an English name.

VASSILY

He had his official designation, but we never encouraged or discouraged him from choosing his own name. I think he was struck by the evocativeness of "Russia Cop" because the name entailed that he was representative of the whole country, and not just a person, an individual. And he was quite right. He wasn't an individual. He was Russia.

CUT TO:

EXT. RED SQUARE - DAY

A reporter holds a mic to a young, attractive woman.

REPORTER

What is your opinion of Russia Cop?

WOMAN BEING INTERVIEWED

I think Russia Cop is doing an amazing thing. He's able to do what ordinary police officers can't do, and I believe with him around, we Russians have a lot more to be optimistic about.

The reporter turns to a middle-aged man standing nearby.

REPORTER

And what about you? What are your thoughts on Russia Cop?

MAN BEING INTERVIEWED

My thoughts are extremely positive. My only concern is that Russia Cop can only be in one place at a time. Why haven't they built more?

REPORTER

How many more should they build?

MAN BEING INTERVIEWED

At least four, I would say.

The reporter faces the camera.

REPORTER

You've heard it here. The people of Moscow have spoken, and they absolutely love Russia Cop. But let's hear from some of his biggest fans.

The camera pans to a group of children. Some are dressed in cheap Russia Cop uniforms.

REPORTER

What do you think about Russia Cop?

The kids cheer and jump enthusiastically.

REPORTER

But those aren't Russia Cop's only admirers.

CUT TO:

EXT. RED SQUARE - DAY

The reporter is speaking with another attractive young woman.

WOMAN BEING INTERVIEWED II

I don't know what it is, but something about him is incredibly sexy. He has all the best qualities you'd want in a Russian man. You know, nowadays too many men are too pretty looking. We often say as long as a man looks better than an ape, that he's passable, but Russia Cop is pure masculinity.

CUT TO:

EXT. RED SQUARE - DAY

WOMAN BEING INTERVIEWED III

I'd (expletive deleted) him.

CUT TO:

INT. PRESS CONFERENCE - DAY

Russia Cop stands at a podium. On either side of him are high-ranking officials and officers. Camera flashes can be seen going off. A member of the press stands to ask a question.

JOURNALIST

Russia Cop, your popularity among women has been steadily rising. The people want to know, what is your ideal woman?

RUSSIA COP

My ideal woman is a patriot.

JOURNALIST

Are you currently dating anyone?

RUSSIA COP

I live to serve. I am Russia Cop.

Major General Cherkassov, a man in his mid-fifties, stands up.

GENERAL CHERKASSOV

Let's look at the statistics. Since Russia Cop appeared on the scene a little over a month ago, violent crimes have gone down thirty percent. Theft has gone down twenty percent, and unpatriotic propaganda has gone down sixty-five percent. All the facts backing up these statistics are available publicly for corroboration. Russia Cop is the future of law enforcement of this country. Russia Cop learns as he works. Expect each of those stats to double, and continue to double, with each consecutive month.

The camera pans back to show several members of the press standing to ask questions. Multiple high-ranking officers take turns answering. The audio is muted as Anna's voice-over kicks in.

ANNA (V.O.)

Generals and colonels sang his praises. They backed up their claims with stats, and letters sent in by the public thanking Russia Cop for his service. But what about ordinary police officers? Those who worked the streets, who were out in the action interacting with citizens? What did they think of Russia Cop?

CUT TO:

EXT. MOSCOW STREET - NIGHT

The camera follows two Russian police officers. They pass several pedestrians. The night is quiet.

ANNA (O.C.)

Is this a typical night for you?

The first officer shrugs. The second officer lights up a cigarette.

POLICE OFFICER II

We walk up and down this street several times a night. It's one of the busier ones. Sometimes we start at the opposite end and make our way this way. Usually it's easier to spot the drunks in the underpass near the metro.

POLICE OFFICER I

There aren't that many public drunks anymore. At least not in this area. Most are in the prison hospital.

ANNA (O.C.)

What kind of crimes do you mostly see these days?

Police Officer I shrugs.

CUT TO:

EXT/INT. PATROL CAR - NIGHT

The two officers sit in their squad car with the windows down. Each one holds a can of beer in his hands.

ANNA (O.C.)

Shouldn't you be out on the streets?

POLICE OFFICER II

Look, we've been walking for forty-five minutes. If something was going to happen, it would have happened by now. Russia Cop has ensured nothing will happen.

CUT TO:

Various shots show police officers, either in squad cars or sitting on park benches, smoking and drinking. Anna's voice-over plays.

ANNA (V.O.)

Similar scenes played out throughout Moscow. Cops who had nothing to do. Sure, their jobs had become infinitely easier, but what would it all lead to?

CUT TO:

INT. VASSILY'S APARTMENT - NIGHT

VASSILY

I won't pretend it didn't feel good. People don't believe me when I say I wasn't in it for the attention, but I really wasn't. I wanted my work to speak for itself. If people appreciated my work and never knew my name, I'd be happy with that. Russia Cop was everywhere. The people loved him. I could go to sleep at night with a clear conscience for the first time in a long time.

ANNA (O.C.)

What happened next?

CUT TO BLACK.

Text appears against a black screen. "It had been six months since Russia Cop made his first appearance. As predicted by General Cherkassov, the decrease in crime was dramatic. The Russian media praised his work and efforts in promoting a more patriotic Russia."

CUT TO:

INT. WITNESS' APARTMENT - NIGHT

From the POV of a cell phone video camera, the witness films what is taking place in the apartment across the street. In the apartment, a young couple can be seen shouting at one another. The man gets closer to the woman, and she is visibly frightened. The witness speaks to someone offscreen.

WITNESS

They're fighting again. Every night now. Sometimes we can even hear them from here. And I thought my upstairs neighbors were bad.

CUT TO:

INT. DARYA AND MIKHAIL'S APARTMENT - NIGHT

From the POV of Darya's cell phone camera, Mikhail, her boyfriend, can be seen coming closer to her. He is fuming.

MIKHAIL

Go ahead and show everyone. They already know what a fucking bitch you are. You think I give a shit if you film this? You lying fucking whore. Go ahead. Show it to your mom and your stupid fucking friends.

DARYA

Get out. Just please leave.

MIKHAIL

Why the hell would I do that? It's my house. Now, for the fiftieth time, when is my fucking dinner going to be ready?

DARYA

Fuck you!

MIKHAIL

What the fuck did you say?

Mikhail gets close to her and she cowers, but she has nowhere to go. With full force, he back-hands her across the face.

MIKHAIL

Say it again, please. Say it again to me.

DARYA

(in tears)

I hate you. I fucking hate you!

Mikhail hits her across the face once more.

DARYA

Help! Somebody help me! Please!

MIKHAIL

You stupid bitch! You're going to wake up all of our fucking neighbors!

Darya continues to scream. Mikhail throws an empty vodka bottle on the ground at her feet. Darya screams louder. At that moment, the door to their apartment bursts open and Russia Cop appears. He is no longer wearing his original uniform. Rather, he is decked out in an Adidas tracksuit.

DARYA

Thank you. Oh, thank God.

RUSSIA COP

Ivanova Darya Petrovna?

DARYA

Yes.

RUSSIA COP

By law of the Russian Federation, I am placing you under arrest. Four neighbors have called citing noise complaints. Three neighbors stated they heard you using curse words. Their children could hear. I am taking you to jail. Mikhail Semyonovich, I apologize for the disturbance.

Russia Cop lifts Darya over his shoulder and carries her out of the apartment.

CUT TO:

EXT. BOULEVARD - DAY

Russia Cop is walking down a busy boulevard. Several reporters attempt to keep up with him and his long strides.

REPORTER II

Can you tell us about this new look, Russia Cop?

Russia Cop stops and stares directly at the camera.

RUSSIA COP

My analytical cognition is second to none. While I may only be six months old, my brain possesses enough processing power to determine that an Adidas tracksuit is the most optimal clothing for the job I do. Since ditching my former attire and adorning this one, my efficacy has gone up two hundred percent.

CUT TO:

EXT. MOSCOW STREET - NIGHT

The two foot cops seen earlier are now patrolling the streets wearing Adidas police uniforms.

CUT TO:

EXT. RED SQUARE-DAY

An enormous crowd gathers to watch the 9 May Victory Day parade in Moscow. There are shots of tanks rolling down the streets and jet fighters soaring through the air above. Children hand bouquets to elderly veterans dressed in their military garb. Accompanying these shots is Anna's voice-over.

ANNA (V.O.)

9 May, Victory Day. While other countries around the world acknowledge 8 May as the day the fascists surrendered, it is recognized on 9 May in Russia. And only in Russia are there parades and celebrations of such proportion. This isn't just a day off for the Russian people. 9 May is a sacred day. It is the day on which Russia defeated fascism. To say Russia holds sacred its role as victor in the

Second World War would be an understatement. This is one of the most important dates in Russian history.

CUT TO:

INT. UNIVERSITY AUDITORIUM - DAY

A World War II veteran sits onstage in front of a crowd of university students. Several professors sit on either side of him. The footage catches him mid-speech.

VETERAN

That was a very hard day. They all were, but that one was nigh impossible. One can go a long time without food. We were already used to that. Even then, I never knew hunger like I did that day. No food, no water. All of our clothes were rotting away. We basically had nothing. But they told us, "Don't fall back. Stop the German advance." And we did that. Day after day. We didn't complain. What saved us and gave us a new spark of hope was the Lend-Lease Act. I never thought I'd be so happy to put on American boots and eat beef out of an American can.

FEMALE PROFESSOR

I must interrupt you. Is it possible you're getting some facts wrong? Maybe I didn't hear you right.

VETERAN

Without the Lend-Lease Act, my entire company would have been gone that day. They saved us.

Several audible "boos" can be heard from the audience. Eventually most of the audience is booing. The female professor stands.

FEMALE PROFESSOR

Clearly there has been some kind of mistake. This old fool clearly doesn't know what he is talking about. There is no evidence of Americans ever providing supplies to our brave Russian defenders. We must kindly ask you to leave.

Before the old man can get up, Russia Cop appears on the stage and proceeds to severely beat the old veteran. The audience merely looks on as the beating unfolds. The old man lays silently and motionlessly on the stage. After a longer than normal pause, Russia Cop drags off his limp body.

CUT TO:

INT. VASSILY'S APARTMENT - NIGHT

ANNA (O.C.)

Did the public perception of Russia Cop change after that day?

VASSILY

People became afraid of him. But I believe many saw that as a positive. Russia has always valued a strong leader or figure. The way the public saw it, if Russia

Cop beat someone to a pulp, then it was in the name of justice.

CUT TO:

INT. MOVIE THEATER CONCESSION STAND - EVENING

From the POV of a cell phone camera, a teen boy films the crowd of people in line in front of him for Instagram Live.

TEEN AT CINEMA

We're about to see some stupid-ass movie right now, isn't that right?

TEEN AT CINEMA'S FRIEND

You're such an idiot.

There is a commotion off-camera. The teen turns his phone to see Russia Cop standing several meters away. Russia Cop seems to be intently staring at something. The camera pans to the concession stand. A teen is ordering a beverage.

TEEN ORDERING BEVERAGE

And one Coke please.

The concession worker hands the teen a Coke. Everyone around him grows quiet. The only oblivious one is the teen with the Coke. Eventually he turns to see Russia Cop giving him a death stare. The teen pulls the Coke toward his chest. Russia Cop reaches for his holster. The teen places the Coke back on the counter. Russia Cop pulls up his hand from the holster.

TEEN ORDERING BEVERAGE

I'll take a kvass instead.

Russia Cop gives a nod of approval.

CUT TO:

EXT. OUTSIDE MCDONALD'S - DAY

There is a big commotion on the streets. People are shoving and shouting. As of yet, the McDonald's is not in frame. The POV is from a pedestrian with a cell phone camera.

ANDREY

Artyom, what's going on?

ARTYOM

I have no idea.

Andrey, filming via cell phone, and Artyom make their way through the crowd. They reach the entrance to the McDonald's, which is being blocked by Russia Cop.

RUSSIA COP

Glorious citizens of the Russian Federation, hear me. Do not put this poison in your bodies. This is the food of fat American invalids. For too long, this food has been allowed to run rampant in our country. No more.

The crowd is screaming and complaining at Russia Cop. McDonald's workers cower in fear behind him.

PEOPLE IN THE CROWD

Let us eat our food!

RUSSIA COP

This is not food. It is American poison. No country has so effectively turned its population into obese whales as the United States. Russia will not go down that route. This is your last warning. You have three seconds to leave the premises. Three, two, one.

Barely after the count of one, Russia Cop grabs the closest person to him, lifts the man above his head, and violently throws him into the crowd. Russia Cop proceeds to beat everyone who is near him. People begin to run, scream, and trample one another. Andrey tries to run and film at the same time. He trips several times. In the distance, Russia Cop can be heard giving commands.

RUSSIA COP (O.C.)

Russian patriots eat at Teremok. Enjoy the taste of Russian heritage at affordable prices.

CUT TO:

EXT. OUTSIDE MCDONALD'S - DAY

We see the aftermath of the previous scene. There are several broken windows and trash and debris on the ground. Some cars have been turned over, and we see ambulances carrying away wounded people.

CUT TO:

INT. VASSILY'S APARTMENT - NIGHT

A close-up shot of Vassily's face. He does not move or speak.

CUT TO:

EXT. SHOPPING CENTER - DAY

People gather, go into, and come out of a large and bustling shopping center. Anna's voice-over plays during the footage.

ANNA (V.O.)

In only half a year, Russia was changed by Russia Cop. Crime rates were down, patriotism was up. But were things truly as bright as they were being portrayed in the media?

The camera pans to a young man with dark hair sitting on a bench outside the shopping center. This is Timur.

CUT TO:

EXT. SHOPPING CENTER - DAY

Timur sits on the bench, looking at the camera.

ANNA (O.C.)

Please tell us your story.

TIMUR

My name is Timur. I'm twenty-eight years old.

ANNA (O.C.)

Where are you from?

TIMUR

I'm from the Republic of Ingushetia, but I've been living in Moscow for nine years.

ANNA

Have you faced many difficulties living in Moscow?

TIMUR

The same types of things many guys from the Northern Caucasus face. At university, they made us fill out forms that asked for details on all of our family members--their addresses, how many live in the households, things like that. I was naive at first and thought all the students had to fill out such forms. Only later did I learn they were only making people from the North Caucasus fill out these forms. They thought we were all terrorists. My sister also goes to university. After the explosion at the airport, everyone she encountered called her a terrorist. At university, the security guard wouldn't let her in, even after she showed her student ID card. He cursed at her and even spit on her. You know, there are so many stereotypes about us. If we aren't terrorists, then we're all thugs and gangsters. We drive fast cars and don't respect women. My friends and I would come to this mall all the time after class and on weekends. We never bothered anyone.

None of us drank. We just liked to gather here. But almost every day, the cops would come and tell us to get lost.

The camera stays on Timur for a time.

CUT TO:

EXT. SHOPPING CENTER - EVENING

The crowds outside the shopping center have grown. Anna's voice-over continues.

ANNA (V.O.)

Many young people from the North Caucasus share similar stories. The Russians often share different stories, echoing his words that Caucasians are loud, aggressive, violent, race cars, and harass women.

CUT TO:

EXT. SHOPPING CENTER - DAY

A young woman is being interviewed by Anna, who is off-camera.

WOMAN BEING INTERVIEWED IV

Personally, I'm thankful Russia Cop cleaned up this area. So often, me and my friends were harassed by those creeps. I almost stopped coming here because the harassment was constant. Yes, I am very grateful Russia Cop got rid of them.

CUT TO:

EXT. SHOPPING CENTER - DAY

Anna is walking side by side with Timur outside the mall.

TIMUR

As you can see, no Caucasian guys anywhere. Russia Cop made sure of that.

ANNA

Everyone says he was only arresting those he saw smoking and drinking in public places.

TIMUR

Do you really believe that? I'll show you something that proves that isn't true. I filmed this myself.

Timur pulls out his cell phone and clicks on a video for Anna to watch.

CUT TO:

EXT. SHOPPING CENTER - EVENING

From Timur's phone, about a dozen Caucasians are standing in a circle around another Caucasian, who is dancing lezginka. The others clap in enthusiastic encouragement. One accompanies with an accordion. From out of nowhere, a small object lands in the center of the circle. It's a flash-bang that goes off and momentarily stuns/blinds the Caucasians. There is a sense of confusion as Timur tries to find out what is going on. When he comes to, he sees Russia Cop beating the Caucasians. Russia Cop takes their limp bodies, throws them in the back of a police van, and locks the door. Timur manages to run away.

CUT TO:

EXT. SHOPPING CENTER - DAY

Timur puts his phone away and turns to Anna.

TIMUR

Tell me, please, where was the smoking and drinking?

The camera stops on Timur's face. This is accompanied by a voice-over from Anna.

ANNA (V.O.)

Timur was right. There was no evidence of any illegal activities. Having said that, there are cases where the Caucasians lived up to the negative stereotypes.

CUT TO:

EXT. PEDESTRIAN WALKWAY - NIGHT

Several Caucasian men are smoking and drinking cigarettes while passersby walk around them. They are listening to Caucasian rap music. A Caucasian not previously seen runs into view, out of breath.

CAUCASIAN WHO IS OUT OF BREATH

Guys! Get out of here! He's coming!

The Caucasians drop their drinks and cigarettes

and run out of frame. The camera pans on the speaker from where the music is coming. A muscular foot smashes down on it. This is Russia Cop's foot.

CUT TO:

EXT. PARKING LOT - NIGHT

A police van with an open back door is in the parking lot. About a dozen Caucasian men sit inside. A fat police officer comes and locks them inside.

FAT POLICE OFFICER

Good riddance.

Russia Cop can be seen in the background observing the situation. After the van drives away, Russia Cop walks to the discarded cigarettes and booze on the floor. He lights up one cigarette, puffs, and seems to inhale euphorically. He then takes a swig from the bottle of vodka. He goes off to sit on a bench, seemingly not realizing he is being filmed, and continues to smoke the cigarette.

CUT TO:

INT. VASSILY'S APARTMENT - NIGHT

Vassily is preparing tea in the kitchen.

ANNA (O.C.)

Were cigarettes and alcohol part of Russia Cop's programming?

VASSILY

Listen to that question. Why would they be? No. And now we still don't know how that footage got out or who was even filming it.

Vassily pours two cups of tea.

FADE TO BLACK.

FADE IN:

EXT. CITY STREET - NIGHT

A young, athletic-looking man approaches a group of youngsters who are smoking and drinking in public. He is the leader of the organization known as the Lion Brigade.

LEADER OF THE LION BRIGADE

Good evening, gentlemen. What are you doing tonight?

DRUNK

What the hell is it to you?

LEADER OF THE LION BRIGADE

Are those alcoholic beverages you're drinking?

Several of the drunks laugh.

DRUNK

Whatever you say, buddy.

LEADER OF THE LION BRIGADE

You are aware that drinking and smoking in public places is against the law of the Russian Federation, are you not? There are children present. You're drinking in full view of parents with their children. Do you really think this is a positive image you're creating?

DRUNK

Who the hell do you think you are?

LEADER OF THE LION BRIGADE

Will you throw your booze and cigarettes in the trash?

DRUNK

Fuck you.

LEADER OF THE LION BRIGADE

Do not curse.

The drunk throws a punch at the leader of the Lion Brigade. A brawl breaks out between the drunks and the members of the Lion Brigade. The camera freezes.

ANNA (V.O.)

This is the Lion Brigade. Founded in 2014, they are a social youth organization that opposes smoking and drinking alcohol in public spaces. They have hundreds of such videos.

Anna's voice-over continues during footage of

other Lion Brigade encounters. Some end in fights. In other videos, the culprits apologize and throw their drinks and cigarettes away.

ANNA (V.O.)

Judging by comments on their YouTube videos, reactions to the organization were mixed. Some saw them as doing good for Russia, whereas others regarded them as nothing more than online vigilantes and hooligans inciting conflict. In either case, most believed they'd become obsolete once Russia Cop came on the scene, but quite the opposite occurred. Instead, more joined their ranks, and they spread throughout the entire expanse of Russia. They also became much bolder in their actions.

CUT TO:

EXT. PARK - NIGHT

A group of Adidas-clad gopniks are drinking beer and smoking in a public park. They are rowdy and laughing loudly. Some of them are alerted when a stranger approaches. It is the leader of the Lion Brigade.

LEADER OF THE LION BRIGADE

Gentlemen, what are you doing tonight?

GOPNIK

Drinking!

The other gopniks laugh.

LEADER OF THE LION BRIGADE

Do you realize drinking in public places is against the law of the Russian Federation?

The gopniks laugh even harder at this. One of the members of the Lion Brigade runs up beside the leader.

THE LION BRIGADE MEMBER

(pointing at the gopniks)

Look!

The camera zooms in on the group of men. Among them is Russia Cop, drinking a bottle of Baltika 9. He is much more bloated than the last time we saw him.

LEADER OF THE LION BRIGADE

Russia Cop, I must inform you that according to the law--

RUSSIA COP

(Interrupting)

No, I must inform you that the law of Russian Soul takes precedent over the law of the Federation. My analyses have concluded that drinking and cigarettes are indeed part of the Russian Soul, and anyone who stands in our way will be savagely beaten. You have exactly three seconds to leave the premises. Three, two, one.

Russia Cop launches his bottle of beer at the leader of the Lion Brigade's head. A brawl breaks out.

CUT TO:

EXT. BOULEVARD - DAY

Russia Cop leads an army of Adidas-clad gopniks behind him down the boulevard. No one stands in their way. They drink and smoke in complete confidence.

ANNA (V.O.)

Russia Cop had his own army now. Nobody stood in their way. When they entered a bar, everyone else vacated. When they crossed the street, the people there crossed to the other side. When convenience stores wouldn't sell them alcohol past eleven p.m., they burned those stores to the ground. And that was only the beginning of their reign of terror.

Intermission

Part Two

EXT. RED SQUARE - DAY

The square is empty.In the first part, it was always bustling with people. Now there is only silence.

CUT TO:

EXT. MOSCOW STREET - DAY

Just like Red Square, a wide boulevard is devoid of people. A stray cat passes across the screen. These shots are accompanied by Anna's voice-over.

ANNA (V.O.)

When I began my conversations with Vassily Gladyshev, Russia Cop had been in operation for two months. With each day, his approval among the Russian populace grew. Now that six months have passed since he was introduced into the world, where do we stand?

CUT TO:

INT. NEWSPAPER NEWSROOM - DAY

A small, cramped newsroom is bustling with activity. Several conversations are taking place between colleagues or over the phone. Multiple phones can be heard going off. The camera pans over to a man between the ages of forty-seven and fifty. He has an intellectual, authoritative look about him and wears glasses. This is Aleksey Pavlovich Proskurin. He is overseeing the work of various others in the office.

ANNA (V.O.)

This is Aleksey Pavlovich Proskurin, a journalist working for the Moscow Gazette and an individual who has developed a reputation for finding himself in troublesome situations. He sat down with me to discuss Russia under Russia Cop.

CUT TO:

INT. ALEKSEY'S OFFICE - DAY

Aleksey sits behind his desk, facing the camera.

ANNA (O.C.)

From the very beginning, you were one of the few journalists who spoke out about their suspicion of Russia Cop. Do you feel those suspicions were founded?

ALEKSEY

Beyond a shadow of a doubt.

ANNA (O.C.)

Do you care to elaborate?

ALEKSEY

The way I saw it, the best-case scenario was that this was a pathetic PR stunt deployed by a desperate, failing inventor, who had used up all his goodwill, and an equally pathetic and ineffective police force.

ANNA (O.C.)

And the worst-case scenario?

ALEKSEY

The worst-case scenario was that Russia Cop would either be a complete success or a complete failure.

ANNA (O.C.)

I don't follow. It would seem Russia Cop was a success. How could both of those scenarios be a worst-case scenario?

ALEKSEY

If by success you mean the creation of an inhumanly strong, possibly unstoppable enforcer of what it deems patriotic on any given day, then yes, what a success. That's a terrifying prospect. Equally terrifying is the more likely outcome, that Vassily Gladyshev actually built something that works but is uncontrollable. Do you think for a second Gladyshev or the police have any control over Russia Cop? What happens if Russia Cop decides to change his ambitions or morals? Last I checked, Russia Cop has his own personal army now.

The camera pans down to reveal that Aleksey is missing his right index finger.

ANNA (O.C.)

Can you tell us how you lost your finger?

CUT TO:

EXT.CITY STREET - NIGHT

From grainy security cam footage, Aleksey can be seen carrying a bag of groceries and making his way to his apartment building. A man approaches him and seems to be asking him a question. Aleksey turns to face the man. At that moment, two men appear from behind Aleksey and begin to beat him with clubs. The beating is severe and relentless. Aleksey falls to the ground, unable to defend himself against his three attackers. They continue to beat him even as he is down. When they walk away, Aleksey is left on the pavement, seemingly dead.

CUT TO:

INT.ALEKSEY'S OFFICE - DAY

ALEKSEY

The beating was so severe, I was put in a medically induced coma. My hands got it the worst, and the finger couldn't be saved.

ANNA (O.C.)

Why did this happen to you?

ALEKSEY

The usual story. I covered and wrote articles about anti-government protests. Look, in this office, we write what other papers won't. We write about corruption. We write about lies. That wasn't the first time my life had been threatened. I wrote from Chechnya. I got off lucky. Two of my colleagues, that I knew personally, were murdered. That is why what we do is so important.

ANNA (O.C.)

Do you view yourself as a martyr?

Aleksey smiles.

ALEKSEY

Let's just say Russia Cop has effectively brought a reign of terror upon our people, but in this office, we are not afraid of him.

CUT TO:

INT. MEETING ROOM - DAY

Aleksey heads a meeting with his staff. What they are saying is inaudible. Anna's voice-over plays during the footage.

ANNA (V.O.)

Attacks on journalists are not uncommon in Russia, but since the emergence of Russia Cop, even the most outspoken journalists had remained silent. I found it strange that Aleksey seemed so calm and confident. When I met with him the following week, he had changed his tune.

CUT TO:

INT.ALEKSEY'S APARTMENT - EVENING

Aleksey paces his kitchen, looking visibly disheveled. His hair is unkempt. He takes quick sips of tea.

ANNA (O.C.)

Aleksey Pavlovich?

He sits down at the kitchen table.

ANNA (V.O.)

What's happened since we last spoke?

ALEKSEY

Do you mind if I smoke?

ANNA (O.C.)

It's your house.

Aleksey lights up a cigarette.

ALEKSEY

I suppose none of this really matters anymore. The day after Russia Cop was announced to the world, we knew something sinister was afoot. A friend, whose name I dare not mention, came to me with a plan. We would do everything in our power to get him a job at the laboratory where Russia Cop was created. We needed to know exactly what went into constructing that creature. The first part of the plan was a success. He was there for several months but was unable to report anything substantial. But then he got bolder and must've found something they didn't want him to find. He's been missing for over a week. When I called his wife, she didn't answer the phone. I went over to their house, and nobody was there. Either they're on the run or, more likely, dead.

ANNA (O.C.)

What will you do?

ALEKSEY

Get me a meeting with Vassily Gladyshev.

ANNA

He hasn't answered any of my calls in over a month. I think he's afraid. I believe you're right. Russia Cop is no longer under his control, or never was.

CUT TO:

EXT. CITY STREET - DAY

Russia Cop leads a column of his Adidas-clad army. There seems to be an endless number of them. The occasional onlooker on either side of the street watches in fear.

CUT TO:

INT. BAR - EVENING

The camera shows an empty bar and a tired, middle-aged bar owner. He wipes down the counter, then turns to the camera.

BAR OWNER

No one comes in anymore.

ANNA (O.C.)

How long has it been like this?

BAR OWNER

Several weeks. At first, the customers were excited when Russia Cop and his army came in. So was I. I considered him a hero. I gave him drinks on the house. But then he started coming back every evening, demanding free drinks for all of his gang. When I told him that was impossible, they harassed not just me, but also my waitresses and bartenders. They scared off all the regulars. Eventually, we ran out of drinks to give them, and they moved on to the next bar. I have nothing left now.

ANNA (O.C.)

I've heard similar stories from other establishments.

BAR OWNER

It's everywhere.

A montage shows various bars. Some have one or two patrons. Others have none at all.

CUT TO:

INT. BAR II - EVENING

A rowdy scene is taking place in the bar. Russia Cop and several members of his army are drinking and eating. There are other patrons in the bar who seem disturbed by the behavior of the Russia Cop army. One of Russia Cop's soldiers is harassing a young waitress who is trying to make her way to the next table. The audio fades as Anna's voice-over can be heard.

ANNA (V.O.)

This place quickly became one of Russia Cop's favorite hangouts. On that particular night, one patron was brave enough to film Russia Cop and his army. Though it is hard to make out, their conversation--what we were able to piece together--is quite disturbing.

The camera zooms in on Russia Cop and the two soldiers sitting nearest him. Their expressions are somber and angry, as opposed to the joyous faces of the others around them.

GOPNIK 1

(Inaudible dialogue) . . . fucking Banderovtsy. (Inaudible dialogue) . . . I'm so sick of those Ukrainian traitors. They think the world is on their side.

GOPNIK 2

Someone ought to smack them around, you know? They need to be taught a lesson.

The camera pans back when Russia Cop looks up from his plate.

ANNA (V.O.)

At this point we couldn't be sure to which Ukrainians they were referring. Had there been an incident with Ukrainians at this bar? It didn't take long to ascertain the meaning behind their words.

FADE TO BLACK.

EXT. CITY STREET/EASTERN UKRAINE - EVENING

An English-language news broadcast with text at the bottom of the screen shows a war-torn city with gray, dilapidated buildings. Sporadic gun-shots and explosions can be heard in the dis-tance. The broadcaster's voice plays over the footage.

ENGLISH-LANGUAGE BROADCASTER

What we are seeing is remarkable. The first reported sightings were given at seven a.m. local time in Luhansk. This footage was recorded just an hour ago.

Several Ukrainian solders run past the camera. They look disheveled and on their last ropes.

UKRAINIAN SOLDIER

Fall back! Fall back! He's coming!

More soldiers run past the camera. The final two are shot in the back and fall dead. The camera pans to reveal Russia Cop, holding his machine gun one-handed (Terminator-style). Russia Cop effortlessly takes out Ukrainian soldiers try-ing to run away. One Ukrainian soldier lobs a grenade at Russia Cop. Russia Cop catches the grenade and tosses it back. The explosion kills the solider. Behind Russia Cop, his army of Adi-das-clad gopniks arrive. Some hold guns, some hold bottles of vodka.

RUSSIA COP

That is for Sevastopol.

CUT TO:

INT. ENGLISH-LANGUAGE NEWSROOM - EVENING

ENGLISH-LANGUAGE BROADCASTER

This just in. The city of Luhansk in eastern Ukraine has capitulated and is now completely under the control of Russia Cop and his army. As of yet, there is no statement from the Kremlin. The German chancellor, set to meet with the Russian president this evening, stated . . .

FADE OUT.

EXT. CITY STREET/EASTERN UKRAINE - NIGHT

Russia Cop and his army drink in the ruins of Luhansk. There is a bonfire and celebratory music playing in the background. They laugh and are in good spirits. Anna's voice-over accompanies the footage.

ANNA (V.O.)

In less than a day, Luhansk was captured by Russia Cop. The following day, they took Donetsk. A rogue army had intervened in an international conflict, and the world watched, stunned. So what was next for the conquering heroes?

One of the drunk gopniks approaches the camera.

DRUNK GOPNIK

We're going to Bali!

Behind him, the other drunk gopniks cheer.

CUT TO:

A montage of shots shows various scenery of Bali. There are beaches, outdoor villas and cafés, warm waters, people surfing and tanning. It couldn't be more picturesque. Anna's voice-over plays during the footage.

ANNA (V.O.)

For years, Bali has been among the most popular tourist destinations for Russians. They arrive en masse, and many end up staying long term. They have not always given locals or other tourists a positive perception of Russians. Then Russia Cop arrived.

CUT TO:

EXT. BALI - DAY

Russia Cop leads his army, marching in formation, down the streets of Bali. On either side are stunned and confused locals, unsure what to make of the scene before them.

CUT TO:

EXT. OUTDOOR RESTAURANT - DAY

Cell phone footage shows a large table where Russia Cop and about a dozen of his men are seated. There are numerous plates of food, bottles of alcohol, and a general mess around them. A confused and stressed waitstaff scurries to and fro, trying to accommodate them all.

RUSSIA COP

I told you fifty times, if you make a single mistake on any of the meals, we will not pay for any of it.

BALI WAITER

Sir! Listen. We did not make mistakes! We do everything you tell us!

RUSSIA COP

Then why was my curry spicy? I said not spicy.

BALI WAITER

That is only way it comes! We told you this yesterday and the day before. Twice you have eaten thousands of dollars' worth of food and did not pay. We cannot tolerate this anymore. You and your friends have to pay.

RUSSIA COP

You listen here. You cannot expect us to pay when the food you've given us was not what we ordered. This is understood worldwide.

BALI WAITER

But you have eaten everything! I'm calling the police!

RUSSIA COP

I am the police!

CUT TO:

EXT. OUTDOOR RESTAURANT - DAY

The restaurant, once bustling with activity, is now burning to the ground, flames tickling the sky.

CUT TO:

EXT. BEACH - DAY

A young and attractive Australian surf instructor sits on a beach chair with the ocean in the background.

SURF INSTRUCTOR

I've been a surf instructor here for the past seven years. I love what I do. I love it here. Everyone who comes here is chill and looking to have a good time. People don't come to Bali to be destructive and start problems. Most of my students are women, and many of them are Russian. Every once in a while, some bloke comes along not really looking to surf but to pick up chicks, but we usually just have a laugh about it. Then Russia Cop and his goons came. They destroyed the beach, lost all my surfboards, and scared my students away. For the first time in almost a decade, I have to go back home. I don't really care about Russia Cop's politics, but come on, mate.

CUT TO:

EXT. BEACHFRONT BAR - DAY

Bangun Pakusadewo, local business owner, is

seen wiping down his counter. The bar is empty. He looks out onto the ocean. Anna's voice-over plays.

ANNA (V.O.)

Business owners were left in a desperate situation, many losing everything. But there were some who saw things differently.

CUT TO:

EXT. BEACHFRONT BAR - DAY

Bangun stands behind his bar counter.

ANNA (O.C.)

Tourism is Bali's largest source of income. Aren't you concerned that Russian tourists will no longer be allowed to the island?

BANGUN

Not at all. In fact, I am quite relieved. Over the years, I've grown sick and tired of these Russians. They act like they own the place, seeing themselves as gods and us as servants. You know, we bend over backward for them, more so than for our own people. It's time we start treating our domestic tourists with respect.

ANNA (O.C.)

Aren't you worried about your business losing money?

BANGUN

Not at all. We will survive. Besides, we'll still have Australian and European tourists, and at least they can speak English. These Russians come to Bali thinking we can speak their language. Good riddance, I say.

FADE TO BLACK.

There is a montage of footage showing local Bali business owners cleaning up restaurants, looking stressed, looking at burned-down buildings, and examining empty beaches. Anna's voice-over plays.

ANNA (V.O.)

In less than a week, Russia Cop effectively killed tourism in Bali. Nine bars and restaurants closed permanently, three were burned to the ground, four surf instructors lost their jobs, and all flights to and from Russia had been canceled. And Russia Cop wasn't done with Bali.

CUT TO:

INT. NGURAH RAI INTERNATIONAL AIRPORT - DAY

Cell phone footage shows Russia Cop and about a dozen of his soldiers checking in for their flight. They carry large, suspicious-looking baggage. The bag checkers look nervous. Several airport staff are seen arguing with each other. A manager approaches Russia Cop and says something inaudible. Russia Cop pulls out his pistol, and the manager cowers like a dog with its tail between its legs. Onlookers watch nervously as Russia Cop places his suspicious luggage on the scale. Anna's voice-over resumes.

ANNA (V.O.)

As soon as this footage went viral, there was speculation as to what exactly it was that Russia Cop was bringing back from Indonesia.

CUT TO:

EXT. CIY STREET/MOSCOW - DAY

People walk the streets of Moscow. They seem to be at ease and are just going about their days. Anna's voice-over plays.

ANNA (V.O.)

When Russia Cop left the country, the people didn't know how to take it. For a couple of days, citizens were unsure whether or not to go back to the way things were. Within three days, bars and cafés were busy again and a sense of normalcy returned. The respite was short-lived, however, as it didn't take long to discover what Russia Cop had brought back from Indonesia.

CUT TO:

INT. CAFÉ - DAY

Cell phone footage shows a group of friends playing a board game and laughing. The other patrons eat and drink coffee in a quaint café. Not much of interest is taking place. Several people are looking at their phones, oblivious to their surroundings. A commotion is heard outside. Patrons turn to the windows. Several people can be seen running by. The person filming the footage gets up, focusing the camera on what is taking place outside. Several more people run by. They are followed by dozens of large orangutans, dressed in Adidas tracksuits. Some are carrying billy clubs. Others are holding pistols. One orangutan stops and pounds on the café window. Several others stop and do the same. The café's patrons erupt, screaming.

CUT TO:

INT. CONVENIENCE STORE - NIGHT

Security footage shows four orangutans filing into a convenience store. They taunt the woman behind the counter. When she pleads with them to leave, they jump up and down, banging on the counter. One orangutan goes through the cold drink section, throwing bottles and cans at employees and customers. Another jumps behind the counter and threatens the cashier. An employee hands a banana to the orangutan behind the counter. The ape eats it and motions with its hand for another. The employee hands over another.

CUT TO:

EXT. BOULEVARD - DAY

Russia Cop's army marches down the street. At the head of the army is the orangutan company. They are followed by the human soldiers. Anna's voice-over plays during the footage.

ANNA (V.O.)

Russia Cop reinforced his army with over two dozen orangutans brought back from Bali. They swiftly developed a taste for violence, while imposing their own brand of law and order.

CUT TO:

EXT. PARK - DAY

A distressed mother has her arms around her two toddlers.

MOTHER

We can't even play in the parks anymore. Three times already, the orangutans came and took off with my babies. Other mothers haven't been so lucky. Have you ever tried to take something out of the grip of one of these apes? They give us no peace. At night, we can hear them screaming and smashing windows. If we can't play in parks, can't trust our children to walk to school on their own, and can't shop without an ape stealing our food and purses, then tell me, please, what can we do? I beg our government, please, please put an end to this.

CUT TO:

INT. ALEKSEY'S OFFICE - DAY

Aleksey slowly drinks a cup of tea. His hair is unkempt, and he hasn't shaved in several days.

ALEKSEY

Has he really not been in contact with you?

ANNA (O.C.)

He has not.

ALEKSEY

No one has seen Vassily Gladyshev in months. None of the high-ranking police officers who worked on the project will speak to me.

ANNA (O.C.)

Have you reached a dead end?

ALEKSEY

Not quite. Have you noticed the disturbing lack of anything coming out of the mouths of ordinary police officers?

ANNA (O.C.)

What are you proposing?

ALEKSEY

Not proposing. I've already started the work. I've been in contact with a street-level cop. He won't give me his name or allow me to show his face, but what he had to say was quite revealing.

CUT TO:

INT. DARK ROOM - EVENING

A man, his face blurred and wearing a police uniform, sits in a dimly lit room. Aleksey is behind the camera.

ALEKSEY (O.C)

Why am I meeting with you?

ANONYMOUS COP

Because my life and the lives of my comrades have become fucking impossible.

ALEKSEY

Tell me what you mean.

ANONYMOUS COP

I'll tell you exactly what I mean. One more week of Russia Cop and the police force of the Russian Federation will not be able to survive.

ALEKSEY (O.C.)

You must elaborate.

ANONYMOUS COP

Are you thick? Money. I'm talking about income. Our salary is lower than worm shit. We survive off our bribes. Every single one of us takes bribes. Any officer who says he doesn't is lying, and everyone is aware of this already, so no point in pretending otherwise.

ALEKSEY (O.C.)

And Russia Cop put an end to cops taking bribes?

ANONYMOUS COP

No, he takes our bribes for himself. But he still makes us do the collecting part. That greedy son of a bitch. What does he need with all that money? My guys can't afford rent or to feed their children. But you know what the biggest insult of all is? He thinks so little of us regular guys, he can't even be bothered to come and get the money himself anymore. Recently he started sending those fucking orangutans to do it. We have to do business with one real mean ape named Cecep. One day, Pasha refused to hand over the money, and Cecep ripped his fucking face off. Now Pasha has to live the rest of his life without a face.

ALEKSEY (O.C.)

I see.

ANONYMOUS COP

You do? How could you? As far as I can tell, you still got a face. More than that, you're one of those fucking journalists.

ALEKSEY (O.C.)

What's that supposed to mean?

ANONYMOUS COP

Exactly what it sounds like. People like you are what's wrong with this country. All you journalists do is write about how terrible everything is here. Where is your pride? Where is your patriotism? I'm a Russian patriot. I did my time in the army. Just looking at you, I know you never served a day in your life.

ALEKSEY (O.C.)

Where does Russia Cop lay his head at night?

ANONYMOUS COP

Nobody knows. Nobody is able to get that close. Nobody but his own soldiers, and even then, only few of them know where he lives. Let me tell you this: he cannot be stopped. It's unlikely we'll be given raises, so our only option seems to be to look for other work.

FADE TO BLACK.

ANNA (V.O.)

Things looked grim. No one seemed to have a solution to the Russia Cop problem. He held the country in his grip. And this was only the beginning . . .

CUT TO:

INT. ALEKSEY'S OFFICE - DAY

Aleksey sits in his office, drinking tea. A colleague runs into the office, panting.

COLLEAGUE

Turn on the television! Quick!

Aleksey turns on the TV. Russia Cop stands behind a podium, giving a speech.

ALEKSEY

Another press conference. What of it? He does a million a week.

COLLEAGUE

This is going out live now, here from Moscow. Now watch this.

The colleague changes the channel to news footage from eastern Ukraine. Russia Cop is seen firing at Ukrainian soldiers who run past the camera.

ALEKSEY

We already know he went there with his army.

COLLEAGUE

You don't understand. This footage is live. This is happening right now.

ALEKSEY

What are you trying to tell me? That Russia Cop is in two places at once? That's ridiculous.

Aleksey grabs the remote and flips it back to the channel showing the press conference.

RUSSIA COP

As many of you have anticipated, I am here today to officially state that I will be running for president of the Russian Federation in the upcoming election, under the banner of the new Russian Soul political party. I will lead Russia to a bright new future.

Aleksey, stunned and staring at the television, slumps in his chair. Eventually, he changes the channel, back to the footage showing war-torn eastern Ukraine. Russia Cop approaches the camera.

RUSSIA COP

You can run as fast and far as you want, but you can never outrun Russia Cop! I will destroy every last one of you!

Aleksey turns off the television.

ALEKSEY

Anna, I suggest you leave Russia immediately.

CUT TO BLACK.

ANNA (V.O.)

After Russia Cop's declaration to run for president, it took only two hours for the president to respond. Even if I wanted to leave Russia, I wouldn't be able to.

CUT TO:

CITY STREET - DAY

Tanks and columns of national guard soldiers line the streets of Moscow. They move forward. The camera pans to reveal that they are approaching Russia Cop, who stands in their path with the uttermost confidence. There is a standoff, during which all goes quiet. The camera pans to Anna.

ANNA

Are you getting this?

The camera pans back to the national guard battalion. At the front of the column stands the colonel. The colonel stares at Russia Cop.

NATIONAL GUARD COLONEL

Open fire!

The tank operators aim their turrets at Russia Cop and begin their bombardment. Several dozen shells hit Russia Cop. A pillar of smoke rises into the air, and Russia Cop becomes obscured by the explosions. The bombardment continues. The ground shakes. Nothing could possibly survive this attack. The tanks cease fire. The world waits as the smoke clears. Russia Cop, unscathed, remains in place. He sports the closest thing to a smirk he has ever shown.

RUSSIA COP

My turn. Attack!

Dozens of orangutans descend from the surrounding rooftops, some landing on national guard soldiers, other apes run and jump toward them, on the attack. Some of the apes are wielding guns, while others throw rocks and other items. The apes are joined by Russia Cop's army of gopniks. A full-blown brawl, at close range, breaks out. Eventually, the two opposing sides venture so close that guns are no longer effective and hand-to-hand combat ensues. The national guard are no match for Russia Cop's combined forces. The battle edges toward Anna and her cameraman. Attack helicopters appear overhead and open fire with miniguns. One helicopter, its machine gun trained on Russia Cop, fires repeatedly, while another launches a barrage of missiles. This time, Russia Cop appears slightly wounded. He has some cuts, but he is still standing.

NATIONAL GUARD OFFICER

Move forward! Finish him off!

A dozen soldiers move forward, firing on Russia Cop as they approach. Russia Cop appears visibly tired. He falls to his knees. The soldiers are now only three meters away. The battle comes to a pause as everyone stops to watch Russia Cop, gasping for breath. Russia Cop coughs violently for a time, clawing at his chest, then a massive lump appears in his throat. Russia Cop's mouth opens, wider than humanly possible, and a giant white egg, larger than a basketball, falls out, landing on the ground at Russia Cop's feet. As Russia Cop catches his breath, those around him look on in shock. The egg rolls and shudders. A fist punches through the shell. A crack spreads across the middle, and the egg breaks open. A miniature Russia Cop, dressed in an Adidas tracksuit, emerges. The soldiers, in a panic, fire at the miniature Russia Cop. Their bullets are ineffective. The miniature Russia Cop grows rapidly to full size and attacks.

NATIONAL GUARD OFFICER

Retreat! Retreat!

The soldiers fall back. The soldiers, along with a crowd of civilians, create a tidal wave of bodies. Anna and her cameraman are caught up in the melee. In their attempt to run, with Anna in the lead, each stumbles multiple times. An orangutan leaps from the roof of a nearby building, landing on the cameraman. The cameraman collapses under his weight. The camera continues rolling from its position on the ground. Anna can be heard screaming while the sounds of the ape beating her cameraman to death can also be heard.

CUT TO BLACK.

A title card reads, "One month later."

FADE IN:

EXT. MOSCOW STREET - DAY

The streets are quiet. Not a soul or car can be seen. The camera traverses the empty streets of Moscow. Anna's voice-over plays.

ANNA (V.O.)

The Battle for Moscow claimed the lives of 125 national guardsman, seventy-six civilians, six orangutans, and my trusted and loyal cameraman, Vladislav Mishkin. Vladislav and I were in the same graduating class, and he has worked with me on every project I've ever been a part of. After his death, I had the chance to call it quits and return home, but I have decided to finish this project in his honor. In the month since the battle, various sects and religious organizations have sprouted up, declaring either Russia Cop an angel sent from God, a new messiah, or God himself, incarnate. One of the sects, the Apes of Destiny, views Russia Cop's orangutan troops as old gods sent from beyond to cleanse the earth, lest they be appeased. Rumor has it that local women have had sexual relations with the apes as a form of appeasement.

CUT TO:

EXT. DARK ALLEYWAY - NIGHT

A woman is seen taking the hand of an orangutan and leading it from the alley into an apartment stairwell. The door closes behind them.

ANNA (V.O.)

These religious organizations have proclaimed Russia Cop as the rightful ruler of the nation and have pledged their support for his presidency. With my new cameraman, Ivan, we meet with Aleksey Proskurin once more.

CUT TO:

INT. ALEKSEY'S OFFICE - DAY

Aleksey, looking even worse off than when we last saw him, smokes a cigarette.

ALEKSEY

I have something to show you.

Aleksey starts a video on his laptop. It shows the Battle for Moscow.

ANNA (O.C.)

I'd rather not see this again.

ALEKSEY

Please, just watch. This clip here shows the ferociousness of the orangutan soldiers. What do you see?

ANNA (O.C.)

They're bloodthirsty. They enjoy violence. Why are you showing me this?

ALEKSEY

Look closely at the apes. Look at the one in the far right corner.

The camera zooms in. Most of the apes are engaged in combat and carnage. They gleefully lob projectiles at their opponents offscreen. The camera finds one ape who is not carrying a weapon. He appears shaken. His head down, he covers his ears with his hands.

ANNA (O.C.)

He seems to be traumatized by the violence.

ALEKSEY

Exactly! The ape's name is Rama. From what I've been able to gather, unlike his brethren, he does not have a taste for violence.

ANNA (O.C.)

What are you getting at?

ALEKSEY

Perhaps, if we can locate Rama, he can lead us to where Russia Cop resides.

ANNA (O.C.)

Say we do. What changes? What good will it do us, knowing where he lives?

ALEKSEY

Listen. There's no tactful way to say this, so I'll just come out with it. Since the beginning of his days, there has been reason to believe that Russia Cop is . . . a homosexual.

ANNA (O.C.)

Aleksey Pavlovich, I must say I'm incredibly disappointed in you. I expect this kind of homophobia from others, but not from you.

ALEKSEY

Wait just a minute. I am not homophobic. I am a champion of gay rights in Russia. I've donated generously to organizations helping gay individuals flee from Chechnya. This is a different matter entirely.

ANNA (O.C.)

Okay. Then help me understand.

ALEKSEY

It caught my attention when Russia Cop refused to give direct answers about his taste in women. Then rumors started to circulate among police officers that he was gay. Everyone took them as jokes at first, but the rumors never stopped. At a certain point, people were afraid to utter them out loud. This isn't about perpetuating Russian homophobia. This is about putting an end to Russia Cop. If we can get definitive proof that Russia Cop is a homosexual and show it to the world, the entire country will turn against him.

ANNA (O.C.)

I don't know. The idea makes me uncomfortable.

ALEKSEY

If you see another alternative, please let me know.

The camera remains on Aleksey as he lights another cigarette.

ANNA (V.O.)

I was uneasy about what Aleksey was proposing. I wanted no part in furthering Russia's views on gay people. I was also uncomfortable being made an accessory. I set out to film a documentary, not to become involved in history-shaping events. But Aleksey seemed determined to show the world that Russia Cop was a homosexual.

CUT TO:

EXT. ALLEY - DAY

Aleksey stands in front of the camera, which is shooting the street from an alley. A line of orangutans marches by.

ALEKSEY

(pointing)

That one there. That's Rama.

Aleksey approaches with caution.

ALEKSEY

Rama.

Several of the apes, who aren't Rama, react to the sound of Aleksey's voice. Rama continues marching forward.

ALEKSEY

Rama!

Even more apes turn to locate where the voice is coming from. Aleksey removes a banana from his jacket pocket and peels it.

ALEKSEY

Rama, I've got something for you.

Rama and another ape break from the line and follow Aleksey into the alley.

ALEKSEY

Get the hell out of here!

Aleksey kicks the other ape in the ass. The other ape returns to the line. Aleksey turns to face Rama.

ALEKSEY

Hi, Rama. I'm Aleksey. It's nice to meet you. Would you like a banana?

Rama holds out his hand to receive the banana.

ALEKSEY

Great. I thought you would. I'd like to be your friend, Rama. Can we be friends?

Rama howls cheerfully.

CUT TO:

INT. ALEKSEY'S APARTMENT - EVENING

Footage shows Rama in Aleksey's apartment, joyfully playing with a puppy and two cats. Aleksey watches on, grinning. Anna's voice-over plays during the footage.

ANNA (V.O.)

Rama got on quickly with Aleksey. He loved his pets and the warm meals he received in Aleksey's home.

CUT TO:

INT. ALEKSEY'S OFFICE - DAY

Aleksey places a small device in Rama's jacket pocket. He then pats Rama on the head.

ALEKSEY

Do you understand the mission, Rama?

Rama opens his mouth in a reassuring manner.

ANNA (O.C.)

What exactly is the mission?

ALEKSEY

After following Rama for over a week, I have witnessed one ape who collects money and hands it over to Russia Cop. I am still unable to get close enough, but with the help of the GPS in Rama's pocket, I'm hoping to get confirmation tonight as to Russia Cop's whereabouts.

ANNA (O.C.)

What then?

ALEKSEY

Then, the plan is to set up hidden cameras and microphones in and around his residence. See what he gets up to when he's not terrorizing the streets.

(turns to Rama)

Rama, I believe in you.

Rama stretches out his long arms to give Aleksey a hug. Aleksey returns the gesture.

A title card reads, "One week later."

INT. UNKOWN APARTMENT - NIGHT

Aleksey is setting up equipment in an apartment. The camera is pointed at a window across the street. A monitor shows the video is good quality.

ALEKSEY

We've been here over two hours now. We believe Russia Cop will be home any minute.

The monitor shows the door opening into the apartment across the street. Russia Cop enters, followed by about a dozen or so men. They move into the kitchen and open bottles of vodka. One of them produces a bag of cocaine and cuts some lines on the counter. They each, including Russia Cop, take turns snorting the lines of coke. One of the men puts on some music (inaudible), and they all start dancing. Several of the men take off their clothes. Russia Cop kneels in front of one of the men and sucks his dick. He then turns to suck the dick of another man, standing behind him. The event develops into a full-blown orgy, with partners occasionally switching.

ALEKSEY

(turning to the camera)

This is what we came here for. We've got it.

Aleksey faces the opposing window once more, taking in the scene before him. Russia Cop, while blowing a man, suddenly locks eyes with Aleksey.

ALEKSEY

Oh shit.

Before Aleksey has time to react, Russia Cop leaps, crashing through his apartment window and soaring over the chasm of the city below before crashing through Aleksey's window. He grabs Aleksey by the neck and effortlessly folds his body into a ball shape.

CUT TO BLACK.

Anna's voice-over plays over a black screen.

ANNA (V.O.)

Aleksey Pavlovich Proskurin was brutally murdered. Aleksey had stated previously that he wasn't afraid to die for the truth, but to me, his death seemed senseless and cruel. I also lost Ivan, my second cameraman, in the incident. Was getting this footage worth the lives of two men? While being recorded, the footage was streaming live on my computer. If I had wanted to, I could have destroyed it. Weighing on my mind, if I were to release it, was the very possible threat to Russia's gay community. Ultimately, in honor of the lives lost, I uploaded the video. Who knew what impact it would have on a world where, each day, it seemed, another new tragedy or history-shaping event occurred? I wish I could say Aleksey and Ivan were the only victims related to the footage, but the body count climbed higher.

CUT TO:

EXT. MONUMENT TO YURI GAGARIN - EVENING

A body hangs by the neck from the Yuri Gagarin monument. The camera zooms in to reveal that it is Rama. A cardboard sign attached to the ape's chest reads, "I am a liar and a traitor."

CUT TO:

INT. PRESS CONFERENCE - DAY

Russia Cop stands behind a podium. On either side of him are armed apes and gopniks.

RUSSIA COP

By now, I am sure you have seen the video that has been making the rounds. Good. Let me be clear. I will one day be president of the Russian Federation. I am Russian Soul. I am Russia. I decide what is what, and I will not rest until every citizen of the Russian Federation has become a homosexual. This is the way of the future, and I assure you, I will see it through.

The apes howl behind him.

FADE TO BLACK.

Anna's voice-over plays over a black screen.

ANNA (V.O.)

What comes next? What will the world look like five years from now? It's difficult to imagine what it might look like tomorrow. With their means of reproduction still unclear, Russia Cops have now been spotted in four different areas of the globe—Ukraine, Estonia, Bali. One has even been spotted in Madagascar. The whereabouts of Vassily Gladyshev, the man responsible for the conception and development of Russia Cop, remains unknown. Nonetheless, the inventor, who had failed so often in the past, unwittingly created invincibility and human flight. We live in the age of Russia Cop.

THE END.

Waiting for Deacon

Saint Petersburg

Pavel Pavlovich Solomka is walking home.

It's five minutes past one in the morning, and he is exhausted. For most he encounters, Friday evening is to be enjoyed—a time to drink with reckless abandon. But not Pavel. He spent the evening at his professor adviser's office, grading papers and assembling his lesson plan for the following week.

To go home. It is the only thing Pavel desires now.

As he turns a corner onto Nevsky Prospekt, he hears a noise. One he can't quite make out. It sounds to him like an excited voice saying, "Might." But the vowel is drawn out and distorted, with a hint of a laugh.

He hears the noise again, realizing it belongs to two voices. Back and forth, Pavel hears what sounds like, "Miiiiight." Or is it "M" followed by the number "8?" Pavel considers his English decent, but he cannot make out what he is hearing.

The source of the noise is revealed when Pavel's path is blocked by two young men, both wearing shorts, flip-flops, and tight-fitting polos. They are clearly intoxicated, and Pavel would prefer not to deal with such individuals on this night.

"Might, youkrawlin tonight?" asks the taller of the two.

Pavel, unable to make sense of what this means, decides it isn't for him and attempts to walk on.

They do not allow him to pass.

"Might, youkrawlin' tonight, or what?" asks the second.

"I'm sorry," Pavel says. "I do not understand."

"Might," the two say in unison.

"What do you need?" Pavel asks.

"Might, what we need is to grab a bevvy and maybe a feed, ya fuckwit."

Pavel struggles to keep up. He does not care for their tone.

"Me'n my might, Kenny, are just a couplabackpackers trynna crawl. We've been crawlin' since Prague and decided to stop ovva in this povvo country. Reckon you know where the crawlin's happening?"

"Where are you from?" Pavel asks.

"Straya, might," says the one not named Kenny.

"Straya?"

"Yeah, might," Kenny says. "Straya."

"Where is this?"

"Might, y'know—Perth, Brisbane." Kenny again.

"Australia?"

"Might!" they both say in unison.

"And why are you here?"

"We're crawlin', ya cunt," says not-Kenny.

"What is this?"

"All right, ya ignorant fuckwit." Kenny rolls his eyes. "It's when you grab a bevvy in a pub, have a laugh, then go to another pub and grab a bevvy there. You like, meet other backpackers, not tourists, but backpackers—real travelers y'know, might? Sometimes there's sheilas with nice bab'eelons. It's never complete without Deacon, though."

Pavel struggles with this word "bab'eelons." Nothing he conjures brings to mind what it can possibly mean.

"Bruce, might." Kenny gives his partner a friendly shove. "Deacon's a legend. One time, Deacon ate nothing but KFC for a whole week."

"Don't talk about keffers, might," Bruce says. "Reckon I might want to grab a feed."

"If I understand correctly," Pavel says, "you want to drink."

Bruce gives a nod. "We go fucking hard no matter what night it is."

"Just go to Dumskaya," Pavel says, pointing. "It's over there."

"Nah, might," Kenny says. "You can't just fuck off. Gotta wait till Deacon gets here. Deacon's a fucking legend."

Another nod from Bruce. "One time I saw Deacon drink a whole six-pack up his arse."

"One time I saw him squeeze six pairs of bab'eelons in one night," Kenny adds.

"All right, ya cunt. One time I saw Deacon pick a fight with the biggest abbo in the room and win."

"All right, might. One time I saw Deacon watch the entire *Frieza Saga* in one day at the library."

"Is Deacon your friend?" Pavel asks.

"Nah, might," Kenny says. "Deacon's a legend. He loves bab'eelons and crawlin'. Loves sheilas. Always banging a different Sheila—between girlfriends, that is."

Pavel doesn't understand how it happens, but soon he finds himself sitting at a bar with the two Australians. Each time he attempts to get up and leave, they force him back down, insisting that he wait for Deacon to get there. It's now half past two in the morning, and Pavel has long since abandoned the idea of getting a good night's sleep. He also never wants to hear the English language again. Whatever it was he studied in school, this is not it. Furthermore, the Australians have no off switch. They haven't stopped talking nearly the entire time, and Pavel can't make any sense of it.

"Got a lighter, might?" Bruce asks Pavel.

Pavel shakes his head.

"Ken, ya cunt. Give us ya lighter."

"You're not getting me lighter, Bruce. Fuck off."

"You be fucked in the head or something. Give us ya lighter."

"Fuck off, might."

"You see, might," Bruce says, "the difference between us 'n yanks is we're like, real travelers, not some fucking tourists."

"We're like, real cultured n' shit," Kenny adds.

Pavel sits, as if paralyzed. Their rudeness is astounding. They shout at waiters from across the room and sit at strangers' tables, uninvited, bringing with them their constant babble of nonsensical events.

Until five in the morning, Pavel waits with the two. He waits right up until the metros open their doors. Deacon never shows. The Australians eventually sod off, seemingly to the next pub. Pavel hopes never to see the likes of them again. Does it even make sense for him to go home at this point? Would he even be able to get in a quick shower and a cup of coffee?

His professor adviser expects him at the university by eight.

Dr. Trinity Barksdale

These sessions are held via Skype

Dr. Barksdale: Good morning. How are you feeling today?

Bruce: Pretty avvo. Just kicking back.

Dr. Barksdale: Are they treating you well there? Are they feeding you enough?

Bruce: They don't even have KFC here.

Dr. Barksdale: I see. Is that important to you?

Bruce: Reckon.

Dr. Barksdale: I see. I notice you haven't been filling out any of your journal entries. Would you like to tell me about that?

Bruce: Fuck you, bitch.

Dr. Barksdale: You seem hostile. Why is that?

Bruce: Because you're like, trying to put your authority on me and shit. I'm like, not so keen on that. Couldn't they have found some Strayan cunt for me to talk with?

Dr. Barksdale: You know, the journal entries don't have to be literature. Just write how you feel. Write the first thing that comes to mind. As little as three sentences would show you put in the effort.

Bruce: I don't want to do it because I don't want to do it! I want to crawl. Why are people always trying to make me do things I don't want to do?

Dr. Barksdale: You mention crawling quite a bit. Is that important to you?

Bruce: Is being retarded important to a fuckwit?

Dr. Barksdale: Tell me about why crawling is so important.

Bruce: I've been crawling for years. I'm like, a real traveler. I'm not like, some American cunt. I've been to like, right dodgy sketch countries like Russia and Budapest.

Dr. Barksdale: I still don't understand why it's so important.

Bruce: Sounds like you've never crawled, sheila.

Dr. Barksdale: Let's talk about Deacon.

Bruce: Deacon's a legend.

Dr. Barksdale: Yes. You've said that during every one of our sessions. But what makes Deacon a legend?

Bruce: Because he like, can drink a lot of Vicky Bazzas and really likes babylons.

Dr. Barksdale: So Deacon is a legend because he likes alcohol and women's breasts slightly more than the rest?

Bruce: Reckon.

Dr. Barksdale: David, I must ask you. You do know Deacon isn't real, right?

Bruce: Who is this David fuckwit? My name is Bruce.

The Rod Juergen Podcast

Somewhere in Texas . . .

Rod Juergen: That's pretty wild. I didn't even know chimps could use those.

Nick: Maaaaaaate.

Rod Juergen: All right, look, you can drop the Australian accent now. Let's be respectful here.

Nick: All right.

Rod Juergen: But I am curious. Why did you do it? Was it meant to be funny?

Nick: It was really funny. It became pretty much a nightly thing for us.

Rod Juergen: But hold on a minute. Why? What was the point?

Nick: Okay, I'll explain. You see, David and I were both part of a study abroad program in Saint Petersburg, Russia. In the winter, we had some time off. I decided to go to the Baltics—you know, Estonia and Latvia. I wasn't expecting much out of the trip, just trying to see places I wouldn't ordinarily go to. It only took about five minutes at the hostel in Tallinn to realize how terrible Australians were.

Rod Juergen: What do you mean?

Nick: I mean, if I had a say in the matter, I wouldn't stay in hostels at all, but they're the cheapest option. I never got into that whole "Oh, we're living under the same roof, we're all travelers, let's all take part in some forced fun and pretend we care about getting to know each other" stuff. But in this hostel, the entire staff were Aussies, as were most of the guests. Within seconds, they established themselves as a party hostel. When I asked for the Wi-Fi password, the main cunt, an Aussie in his mid-to-late thirties, laughed and said, "Mate, you're gonna be too busy crawlin' to have time to answer your little Facebook messages." That's when I learned about the Australian love of pub crawls. It's also when I realized that that was the extent of who Australians are as people.

Rod Juergen: What are you talking about, man? I love Australians. They're some of the nicest, funnest people I've ever met. I've always had a great time traveling in Australia.

Nick: I don't know. I've never even been to Australia, but these guys at the hostels, they were all dreadful. They forced us to play a bunch of high school drinking games. Stuff like Never Have I Ever. In the beginning, I thought they were putting on an act for the tourists, but no, that's just who they are. The entire game, all they could talk about was how much they like sex and drinking booze. Keep in mind, these guys were all in their thirties. Whenever any question arose about a past experience, every example they gave took place on a pub crawl. When talking about a pub crawl in Budapest, suddenly that story would turn into talking about a pub crawl in Prague. When we actually went out on a pub crawl in Tallinn, they ran into other Aussies and reminisced about other pub crawls they'd been on in Europe. These guys, they've been living in Eastern Europe for years, but they don't know a single word of the local language. They don't have any local friends. They just go on pub crawls and meet other Aussies.

Rod Juergen: What's wrong with that? They seem like guys having fun and doing what they like.

Nick: It just rubbed me the wrong way. Americans get a bad rap wherever they travel. I couldn't help but feel that Australians were easily a thousand times worse. After I got back to Saint Petersburg, I was just so frustrated. I had all these thoughts about Australians and how awful they were. Then I learned David had stayed at the same hostels and had the exact same experience I had. Do you know how cathartic it was to go back and forth with someone else about how much we disliked Australians? During our discussions, we found we were both pretty good at doing the accent.

Rod Juergen: Your Australian accent really isn't that good, bro.

Nick: Worked for us. We made ourselves laugh. Then, eventually, it became natural. We couldn't stop doing it. Every time we went out drinking in Saint Petersburg, we weren't merely *pretending* to be Aussies, we *were* Aussies. Thing is, Russians can be pretty annoying. Whenever they hear people speaking English, they want to harass you and bombard you with questions. They want to know everything about America. While it might be interesting for them, it's boring as shit for us. The first time Russians showed an interest in us, it was kind of cool. But after the seventeenth and eighteenth times, you grow tired of it. Sometimes you just want to have dinner with a friend, in peace, without some Russian showing up at your table, uninvited, bombarding you with inane questions. As Aussies, we could flip the script. We could say and get away with whatever we wanted. Do you know how many times we encountered skinheads and nationalists and the mere fact that we were Australian saved our lives?

Rod Juergen: Fact? From what I gather, it sounds to me like you guys just went around harassing people. I don't see anything funny about that.

Nick: It had to be done. Our revenge against the Russian Soul.

Rod Juergen: What does that mean?

Nick: We introduced a bit of Australian Soul into the mix.

Rod Juergen: I don't know, man. It seems to me you're trying to put this guy's bad behavior and terrible decision-making on Russia.

Nick: I mean, no. I wouldn't say that. Bruce wouldn't say that either. He'd say he's a master of his own destiny. And that he doesn't like when people put their authority on him.

Rod Juergen: So you guys go around bothering people, pretending to be Australian. What led to David's arrest?

Nick: We decided to crawl our way across Russia. Once we'd made our way east, David said we should crawl to North Korea.

Rod Juergen: You weren't serious.

Nick: Bruce and Kenny were absolutely serious. I'm trying to tell you. We weren't pretending to be Australian, we *were* Australian. Bruce and Kenny, they thought crawling to North Korea was a great idea.

Rod Juergen: Why weren't you there with him?

Nick: We decided to crawl a bit before crossing the border. We had like, twelve beers each. We were waiting for Deacon. Once Deacon didn't show up, Bruce, I mean David, decided to just get going. I told him to wait up, but I guess he didn't hear me. I ran to the bathroom and threw up all over the place. When I came out, David was gone.

Rod Juergen: David crossed into North Korea, somehow bypassing all the checkpoints.

Nick: He did. He's an expert crawler.

Rod Juergen: But he didn't make it far. They arrested him.

Nick: They arrested him. I mean, the rest is history. An American sneaks into North Korea, of course it's going to make international headlines and cause a ruckus.

Rod Juergen: But he refused to admit he was American. Even during all the interrogations and conferences, he stayed Bruce the entire time. Even when his parents pleaded with him, he wouldn't break character. Did you see the video of his mother pleading before the UN? Fucking heartbreaking. And her—sorry to say—dipshit son claimed he didn't know who she was.

Nick: That's how determined he was to crawl in North Korea. Multiple organizations reached out to him, imploring him to admit the truth. Hell, even the North Korean government was determined to get him to admit the truth. They even allowed an appointed therapist to speak with him via Skype. The therapist tried her best, but he wouldn't budge.

Rod Juergen: Were you allowed to talk to him?

Nick: I was.

Rod Juergen: So?

Nick: Well, here's the thing: The moment you get the two of us talking, we can't not do the accent. Bruce and Kenny take over. Of course, I wanted to save my friend, but Kenny, the pub crawler, he was in complete support of Bruce. To him, Bruce was a legend, up there with Deacon.

Rod Juergen: You fucking idiot. Don't you realize you got your friend killed?

Nick: Look, Bruce was willing to die for the crawl.

Rod Juergen: I'm going to play a video. Tell me how you feel when you watch it.

Death Sentence

Pyongyang

North Korean Official: The American has been found guilty of espionage, smuggling in of contraband items, lying to elected officials, and impersonating a foreign national. We have given him ample opportunity to repent, so that his life may be spared. Even after two years in captivity, he has refused. His time at our reeducation center has proven unsuccessful. For his crimes and refusal to cooperate, he is sentenced to die. His date of execution happens to coincide with the launch of our new Juche Peoples' Rocket. As a means of execution, David will be fastened to the outside of the rocket and executed by means of accompanying the rocket as it is launched into the sun. Thank you, Dear Leader.

David's Last Words

"My mate Kenny once asked me if we'd ever run out of places to crawl. I replied, 'Mate, crawlin' is eternal. If, on this earthly realm, we crawl everywhere there is to crawl, then I will crawl on the fucking sun.'

"Today I'm being given that opportunity. I will crawl where no bogan ever has. I have no regrets. I've crawled in North Korea, and soon, I'll be crawlin' in space. When the Asian blokes told me where I'd be going, I had only one question: 'Is the beer cold on the sun?' So, fuck off ya cunts, I've got some crawlin' to do. Deacon, I'll see you there, you cunt."

Afterword

Artistic liberties have been taken with the geography and establishments mentioned in the city of Volgograd. While certain bridges and bars mentioned in the story do exist, some of them don't quite match their real-world counterparts. The Black Dog in the story, for example, is an amalgamation of bars in Volgograd and Moscow. Any other geographical goofs that may appear in the story are purely mistakes on the part of the author. The story presented in this collection is in no way a biographical work on the rock legend Viktor Tsoi. Having said that, I will use any opportunity to expose people to the joy that is his music.

Acknowledgements

First and foremost, a very special thanks to my dear friend, Sasha Amelchenko. I'm not sure what I did to deserve you, but none of this would have been possible without you. Thanks must be given to Matt Dubow and Anne Collette. I don't know what compels you to do it, but the two of you are always willing to read my work in its earliest and roughest form. Thanks also must be given to Melissa del Bosque, Marcus Urango, Kai Suzuki, Michael Pesoli, Yoko Hori, Aiko Anna, editors Eric Wyman and Kyle Fager, and to the amazing artist, Alfred Obare. Without the help, insight, and suggestions from these people, this book would not exist.

CPSIA information can be obtained
at www.ICGtesting.com
Printed in the USA
BVHW032057130322
631379BV00006B/51

9 781736 277317